With what nervous anticipation Mercy awaited Miles' arrival; the sound of horses' hooves on the sparkling gravel or a sharp knock on the front door seemed to stop her heart beating.

Matthew looked around for Mercy and saw her descending the stairs, resplendent in a new white crinoline trimmed with hyacinth blue ribbons the colour of her eyes. Her chestnut hair, in spite of vigorous brushing tumbled about her shoulders. Even as the astonishing thought struck him of how beautiful she had become, a thunderous knocking on the front door sent Archer swiftly running.

There stood Miles, resplendent in his scarlet cloak, dark handsome eyes sparkling with pleasure.

As he stepped into the hall dozens of eyes watched, and all conversation flagged. The orchestra tinkled away thinly in the background as Matthew came forward smiling.

But Miles looked to the stairs where the tremulous figure of Mercy stood, flushed and covered with confusion. He had eyes for no one but her, and he strode across and lifted her bodily down. He took both her hands before the astonished crowd and gazed into her eyes. A breathless stillness encompassed them both.

"I told you I would return," he whispered softly.

the House in Holly Walk

by

Dorothy Wakeley

ace books
A Division of Charter Communications Inc.
A GROSSET & DUNLAP COMPANY
360 Park Avenue South
New York, New York 10010

THE HOUSE IN HOLLY WALK

Copyright © 1978 by Dorothy Wakeley

All rights reserved. No part of this book may be reproduced in any form or by any means, except for the inclusion of brief quotations in a review, without permission in writing from the publisher.

All characters in this book are fictitious. Any resemblance to actual persons, living or dead, is purely coincidental.

An ACE Book
by arrangement with Robert Hale Ltd.

Published simultaneously in Canada

ONE

It was soon after dawn when Mercy awoke. A pale splash of sunlight peeped through the curtains and early summer sounds were heard from joyous birds. She could hear the clack of horses in the stable yard, and the creak of harness meant the already shining leather was being polished in preparation for this blissful day.

She knew she must stifle the impulse to rush along to her elder sister's room. To creep in and discover if Faith, today's bride, was also stirring in anticipation of the coming event.

Mercy's thoughts turned to her eldest sister. The house would be different after today, for Faith had, with her quiet serenity since their mother's death, kept the family firmly together with a placid composure that belied her twenty-two years. Papa would of course miss Faith sitting serenely at the head of his table. He had taken as his due the young subdued girl deputising for his wife, long since dead, and, when more than a year ago Alfred Tafler, the curate of All Souls, had begun to take an interest in her, he had as a matter of course strongly disapproved, never entertaining the idea of marriage for his eldest daughter. She was too useful to him and why should she want to leave the pleasant life in Holly Walk? The younger girls he would naturally expect to marry at a later date, but Faith was too valuable to his comfort, and the idea of a curate preposterous.

However, the curate was a determined young man and although he treated Papa with respect he still sought out Faith at every opportunity. She, a gentle shy young woman, had from the age of fifteen cared for her father and three young sisters. There were five indoor servants to carry out the menial tasks, but their well-being, in addition to the immediate family, must be considered and it had all fallen on Faith's slender shoulders. It seemed to Mercy, whose memory of her mother was a languidly reclining figure continually ill, that Faith had never been young. Her long face framed by soft brown hair was always serious with concern for the family and staff in her father's house. She believed she was destined to be a spinster all her life, and when suddenly becoming aware of an admirer, was disconcerted but enchanted. She appeared to bloom like a flower in the sun, her plain little face took on a rosy glow whenever Alfred's name cropped up or he unexpectedly called on some flimsy excuse at the house. It was a source of amazement to them all that docile Faith firmly defied Papa's wishes and accepted Alfred's proposal without even a fitting time for reflection.

THE HOUSE IN HOLLY WALK

By this time the old vicar of All Souls had succumbed to a severe winter in his cold dark vicarage and the curate was promoted to the living. This encouraging news caused Papa to capitulate, and wishing to appear benevolent he did so gracefully. The date had then been fixed for this May morning of 1852.

The sun rose higher, enticing sixteen-year-old Mercy from her bed to fling wide the curtains and look out onto the garden. Newly washed with dew, trees bent low with blossom, it looked already bridal in its summer glory.

Gyp was barking excitedly as a gardener, with angry shouts, chased him off the freshly cut grass. She laughed with pleasure to see her little dog insolently dodging a clod of earth. Feeling she would burst with exuberant spirits, she hurried along to the room shared by her other two sisters, Hope and Charity.

"Wake up!" she cried, pulling aside the curtains and letting in the morning light. "It is the most beautiful day."

A head of palest gold appeared, and two startled blue eyes peeped out of the large bed.

"Oh, Mercy, it's you. What time is it?"

"Time you were out of bed! Where's Charity?"

"She went down hours ago feeling very full of her own importance and taking over her responsibilities from this very moment. She says she won't let Faith do a single thing today except compose herself for the service and look beautiful for her bridegroom, as beautiful as she can look of course." Hope smiled smugly, preening with a vanity allowed to the beauty of the family.

"Every girl looks lovely on her wedding day," Mercy retorted sharply, "and don't let me find you primping yourself before everyone, trying to eclipse the bride. Your day will come, and mine too one day I hope, so just behave."

Hope laughed and jumping out of bed twirled her sister round the room.

"You little goose, Mercy, of course I won't spoil Faith's day and I hope she will be very happy in spite of marrying an old stick in the mud like Alfred." She paused. "The man I marry," she continued, "must be tall and strong and very, very handsome. An army man, I think."

Mercy looked suspiciously at the overbright eyes.

"You are not thinking of course about a certain young officer here to attend his cousin's wedding?" she asked innocently.

"If you mean Harry Betteridge, I certainly am not!" was the emphatic reply. "Anyway he is not strictly an army man, simply attached to his college platoon at Oxford. That fancy uniform was made to impress." Hope paused to reflect. "He is exceptionally handsome though, you must admit Mercy. I just cannot believe that he and Alfred are cousins, they are such complete opposites."

Mercy nodded, changing the subject.

"What about Aunt Lydia and her life abroad? She makes it sound so exciting."

"I know, and her *gowns*. What about the lilac silk with that enormous skirt? How she manages to enter a carriage I can't imagine."

They giggled together, then Mercy sighed resignedly.

"I would love to travel and see all the exotic places Aunt Lydia simply takes for granted. But I am so glad she stayed for the wedding. Faith would have been dreadfully disappointed had she sailed for India before today. Uncle Charles must be very kind to allow her so much freedom."

"Oh pooh! She only had to suggest she would follow him out to India when it suited her and the poor man simply agreed. I admire Aunt Lydia tremendously. She knows exactly how to deal with men. She has such style."

Two pairs of wistful eyes met.

"I have a feeling our bridesmaids' dresses are going to look very out-moded against Aunty Lydia's newest creation." Hope pouted, then continued reflectively, "I wonder how Faith feels. Just imagine, last night for the very last time she slept alone. It must be divinely exciting sharing a bed with a man." A shiver of alarm ran through her slender frame. "I wish someone would tell me what to expect. Do you think Faith knows?"

"Somehow I think Aunt Lydia has seen to that," Mercy replied wisely. "I saw them disappear together late last night. Besides, Alfred seems very kind; I am sure he wouldn't do anything to frighten her."

"Well, I don't know. I overheard Cook telling Amy that all men are beasts under the blanket. And anyway, babies aren't made simply by kissing you know. There must be something very improper about it or there wouldn't be all this secrecy. I intend to find out very soon myself. When Faith has been married a short while I shall ask her."

Wishing life were not quite so complicated, Mercy moved to the door. "Do hurry and dress," she urged. "I don't want to miss a single minute of today. It will be so nice to have the house full of people."

"If only there were a few new faces. Everyone is so familiar. All Papa's old friends and associates, hardly anyone under forty. Have you ever considered, Mercy, how very few friends of our own age we have? Oh I know old school friends like Alice and Nancy Ingram and the Moreton girls are coming but there is simply not a single male of reasonable age invited. How can we possibly marry if we are never introduced to eligible men?"

"Well, Percy Adler is coming ... you know how he flattered you at the Moreton's Christmas ball. And Alfred's dashing cousin Harry has obviously impressed you."

"Percy Adler!" Hope exploded. "That chinless nincompoop." She wrinkled her nose in disgust. "And as for Harry Betteridge, we have scarcely exchanged a word, although of course I intend to rectify that today."

Mercy laughed as she left her sister's room and hastened away to dress. She felt that Charity might need her help in the dozens of last minute things needing attention. She must also control

Gyp and groom him into presentable condition. Papa was extremely strict about his appearance in the presence of visitors. She sang softly with the sheer joy of youth, and appreciation of the golden sun sent solely, she was sure, for the bride's benefit.

Matthew Glover was up and partly dressed when the hot water arrived a little after seven o'clock.

"You are ten minutes late, Archer," he rebuked sharply.

"I'm sorry, sir. There's a bit of confusion in the kitchen this morning."

Matthew gave a non-committal grunt. Although Archer's duties included supervising the pantry, attending the door, and generally managing cook, parlour maid, housemaid and other indoor staff, it was understood that first thing in the morning and on retiring his master's welfare was Archer's sole purpose. He was, strictly speaking, neither valet nor butler, but a superior being of long standing service, ruling his own domain with an indomitable hand. With the exception of Cook, the whole domestic staff treated him with awe and respect.

Archer was undisturbed by his master's short rebuke. After many years service he knew, perhaps better than anyone, that the haughty domineering manner hid a generous, warm heart. Stern and austere when necessary, a temper quick to arise and as quick to subside, belied a keen sense of justice and a deep abiding devotion to his family and dependents. Master and servant understood each other perfectly, each respecting the other's good points and each keeping meticulously to his place.

Matthew waved a hand indicating that shaving was to proceed, his thoughts preoccupied.

When he had given consent to his eldest daughter's marriage he had failed to realise quite how much the event would upset the even tempo of the household. Naturally he told himself the happiness of Faith was to him a primary concern. It was perhaps a little disappointing she had chosen Alfred Tafler. But there had hardly been a rush for her hand, and although a dear, good girl, even the most generous person would never consider her a beauty. He felt he had treated the young couple generously however by presenting them with a handsome dowry. Enough at least to enliven the interior of that dreary vicarage beyond recognition, and leave a little over for any future expenses.

His second daughter, Hope, should by right inherit the household tasks, but Matthew, smiling indulgently at the thought of his favourite child, realised how inadequately she would cope. Such a dear little thing with that wealth of fair hair, and blue eyes to melt the most hardened heart. She had a way of beguiling him with a toss of her wayward head, but her firm refusal to accept the vacated role was regarded with distinct disapproval by his female relations. A hint of tears on the fluttering

THE HOUSE IN HOLLY WALK

lashes however had caused him to turn with little consideration and perhaps no regret to Charity, his third daughter.

Charity was sensible enough although inclined with some frequency to daydream. He knew less of her character than the others, he reflected, for she was a queer secretive girl. He also had some misgivings on the extremely advanced views she had occasionally expressed. He would have to curb her outspoken remarks in future if she was to sit by his side and support him at table when entertaining friends. There should however be no difficulty for she was not the type to waste words on frivolities. Her small, neat figure and usually quiet manner would grace most occasions, and in spite of her pale delicate face causing him some concern—she was so like her mother—the large dark eyes were alert with intelligence. Matthew had not the slightest doubt that Charity would, in a short space of time, be as competently in charge of his home as her sister had been.

The bone of contention in Matthew's life was the plague of daughters thrust upon him. Why, when he wanted a son so badly, was every child of his a girl? After the birth of Mercy sixteen years ago his wife had given up hope, and over nine years her health had slowly deteriorated. The possibility of other children gone, she became a semi-invalid and during the latter years she and Matthew ceased to have any physical contact at all. This was no great hardship to Matthew. He was not a particularly sensual man, and how he learned to control his natural feelings was firmly his own affair.

He had many advanced ideas for a man of the times. Morning prayers had, during the last year, been dispensed with entirely. That the girls knelt in prayer every night on retiring however, was firmly understood, and the family as a whole attended Church unfailingly twice on Sundays. Matthew, in spite of his several eccentricities had earned the respect and admiration of the community in this attractive, flourishing Midland town, which by sheer hard work and interest in his fellow men he had helped to create.

Fleetingly he thought of his dead wife. Poor Cissie, how she would have enjoyed today and the delight of her eldest child's wedding. She had in her own way loved all the girls and treated them as pretty playthings. He had felt a little foolish in allowing her to indulge in their pious and sentimental names. His sister Lydia wickedly observed that at the delivery of his last daughter, the midwife, knowing how ardently Matthew prayed for a son, had exclaimed in despair, "Mercy, another girl." Matthew emphatically denied this story in connection with the child's name.

At the thought of his sister, Matthew felt a surge of affection. It was fortunate she was able to stay for the wedding; the girls were extremely fond of her, she was such wonderful company. At times he felt concern at her way of life, which he considered unfeminine and slightly shocking in a woman. Her warm generosity and complete lack of affection, however, outweighed her modern and perhaps rather flighty ideas, so he accepted her just as she was at forty-five years, gay, charming and extremely fashionable. Married to a wealthy peer who adored her, how could she be otherwise? She led a very varied life, had travelled extensively and was due to sail for India to join her officer husband in the near future. The girls hung on her words, listening avidly to her amusing tales and he was occasionally a little disturbed at Hope who was very impressionable. The way she gazed at her aunt in adoration and stared with open envy at her elegance he found disconcerting.

As he dressed Matthew glanced out of the window in satisfaction. In what profusion the lilac and laburnum bloomed this year, and early mist now dispersing over the well-kept garden gave promise of a warm sunny day.

Suddenly a flutter of white petticoats swept across his vision and shrill cries were mingled with the excited barking from a flurry of black and tan fur. Matthew frowned and pursed his lips in annoyance. He really must be more severe with Mercy and curb this unseemly behaviour. She must learn a little decorum now that she was well over sixteen years, and he must forbid her to rush about so scandalously in her underwear like a ragamuffin. Although she hadn't the looks of the fairer Hope, he felt there were possibilities in her large violet eyes and rich chestnut hair which glinted in the sun as she flew giddily through the rhododendron bushes. She had a sweet nature, enveloping everyone with a warm generous love and in spite of feeling it his duty to curb her high spirits, this, he would not wish to change.

Happiness flowed through his house and he had enough insight to see it. Never, within limits of propriety, had he forbidden the girls to indulge their natural emotions. There was nothing he liked more than to hear laughter on the stairs, light skipping feet, and the sight of the fresh bright faces of his family before him. He kept them as beautifully dressed as the local shops allowed, feeling loyally that the local tradesmen should be encouraged if the prosperity of the town was to be developed. Occasionally the prim little daughters of acquaintances would cause some heart-searching and compel him to view with alarm the high spirits of his own family. For a few days rules of stern discipline would then be enforced. Nevertheless, within a very short time things were back to normal, for an uncomfortable houseful of subdued little mice suited Matthew not at all.

Dressed for the wedding, Matthew left his room and descended the wide flower-decked staircase. Enormous urns of white lilac graced both landings and their delicate scent wafted upwards from the hall below.

Polly, the down-stairs maid, scuttling across the dining-room, glimpsed him with awe and admiration. He seemed like a god to her, his tall well-set figure erect, thick chestnut hair and full beard gleaming in the sun from the landing window. From his immaculate trousers and lavender waistcoat to the severe black tail-coat he was perfection.

As he walked along the corridor Matthew glanced critically into the upstairs drawing-room which was large and graciously appointed. Everything seemed in order from the small overcrowded tables to the handsome crimson loving-seat. Heaped on the grand piano—on which the girls indifferently played—were bowls of colourful spring flowers.

Descending into the hall, a sudden glimpse of himself in the lofty mirror gave Matthew immense satisfaction. He was never one to do things by halves and although the guest list of fifty was comparatively small, many were influential citizens of the town. It was quite unnecessary to wish to impress since twenty-three years had firmly established him in the local community, but he had enough human failings to wish to stand well among important associates and a certain pride he felt was forgivable. After all it was no mean achievement for the younger son of a Yorkshire farmer to make his way so successfully in the property business. Admittedly some credit was due to his father, a wise and prosperous man. He had educated three sons to the best of his ability and given them a fair choice of careers. When Matthew had chosen to become a property dealer he was apprenticed to a well known business in York, where quick wits and shrewdness took him swiftly ahead. On reaching his twenty-ninth year he was prepared to leave the North and investigate the Midlands, where he later bought himself a partnership in an old established firm.

Now at fifty-six he was a senior partner, and in a slightly self-satisfied way he viewed with pride his reasonable wealth.

The house in Holly Walk was well back from the road and half hidden behind graceful birches. A wide curving drive allowed the carriage ample room to manoeuvre and rest before the Corinthian pillars of the front porch. It was an imposing house with a broad white façade and an elegant air of Georgian simplicity. Whenever he surveyed his property Matthew congratulated himself on his own ingenuity at snapping up this house when it came on the market, albeit neglected and almost derelict in the early days of his marriage. His own astuteness, time and money spent on the place had brought its just rewards. There were few other establishments in the town to compare with its imposing well-kept gardens and general air of good taste. Quite a few tentative offers of purchase had come his way. But this house was Matthew's pride and joy and he hoped the start of a family inheritance.

Although there was no son, one day male grandchildren would appear, of that he had no doubt, and he intended to prepare for such an occasion with foresight and determination.

TWO

THE GARDENS and flagged terraces in Holly Walk displayed a riot of colour, as the ladies twirled their frilled parasols to the swish of satin gowns and discussed with the gentlemen how successful was the marriage service.

The bride, flushed, her demure eyes bright, had never been so important. A head-dress of pale roses nestled like a crown on the soft brown hair drawn severely over her ears. She had refused, in spite of ardent pleadings on the part of her younger sisters, to have the front frizzled into curls, and her wedding gown looped with cream roses was far simpler than the flounced gauze worn by the bridesmaids. She glanced slightly nervously at the solemn young man at her side, but a smile from his kind earnest face was reassuring.

Hope, the dancing blue ribbons on her dress competing with the brilliance of her eyes, gazed enviously at her sister.

"Your voice was so clear, Faith. We heard every word, which is more than I can say of Alfred." She laughed, her eyes skimming over her new brother-in-law to peep at a tall fair-haired young man standing immediately behind him. He was dressed in the magnificent blue and red uniform of the Guards and he watched her coolly and appraisingly. Hope dropped her eyes coquettishly, only half listening to the babble of voices around her.

"You are always so serene, darling Faith, and with Papa at your side, looking so distinguished, it must have helped a lot."

"Oh, it did," murmured the bride, "but I really felt uncommonly nervous and naturally it was more than I dared do to show it."

Her voice dropped and she leaned towards Charity in the crowd. "If I had faltered Papa would never have forgiven me, I am sure."

She and Charity smiled at each other with affection. Perhaps only Charity, who was wiser than most, realised how thankful Faith was to relinquish the responsibilites of this household. She appreciated that in his own eyes Matthew was a lenient and indulgent father, but she, knowing few other men in his position, had very little idea how very strict and dogmatic the Master of the house could be. She only knew that in her natural timidity his exorbitant manner and explosive habits often brought her to near physical collapse, and any confidence she might have had vanished like a puff of smoke. Oh the joy of leaving it all behind, of living in her own home, which in spite of their efforts at restoration was still the dark decaying old vicarage of All Souls. But what heaven it would be to awake to a tranquil day with just one unskilled little maid to help her run the house. With only Alfred to satisfy, solid, calm and understanding. She felt a twinge of conscience for so joyfully handing over her former unenviable role to Charity. But, knowing how firmly the square determined little chin on the face before her could set on occasion, her guilt faded. That it could deal with Papa and his fastidious foibles when necessary Faith had no doubt.

Suddenly a bonnet billowing with net appeared and Aunt Lydia advanced, cool and assured, with two middle-aged gentlemen dancing attendance.

"Why, Faith, in spite of your guests, I do believe you are daydreaming. I hope they are bright dreams for the future. I wish you so much happiness, darling."

"Thank you, Aunt Lydia. I am so grateful for the lovely day and to everyone concerned with making the last occasion in my old home so successful."

"I am quite sure you had a hand in organising it yourself, my dear. I have never known a bride arrange her own wedding so beautifully. You will enjoy returning here as an honoured guest I feel sure, and there will be other weddings to look forward to in the future." She turned to the bridegroom. "Now, Alfred, take your bride into circulation, so many friends are waiting to greet you."

Smiling fondly as the young couple moved away, Lydia Asterling felt relief at the girl's obvious happiness. Poor Faith, life had been too full of responsibility until now and although she might never know with Alfred much gay abandon, at least she had thrown off the shackles of her father's house and the trials of pleasing an exacting parent. Whatever troubles she had in the future would be of her own making and not thrust indiscriminately upon her. It was a great pity her brother had not made a second marriage thus allowing the girls more outside freedom. It disturbed her to think another one was to step into Faith's shoes and fare in the same manner. She herself had several times suggested a housekeeper, but Matthew had protested indignantly. The house was already overrun with females, he declared adamantly. Surely one of his brood was capable of tending his needs with the adequate servants provided.

The welfare of the guests uppermost in her mind, Lydia helped the younger girls in catering for their comforts. She thought they all looked very pretty in their dainty bridesmaids' dresses. Hope, the brilliant butterfly, was managing to flash more ankle, lower her neckline and tip her bonnet more extravagantly than anyone else in sight. This still could not, however, subdue the dancing light in Mercy's eyes, or dull the bloom of her extreme youth. Charity needed no encouragement in her duties. She moved solemnly among the crowd, treating the old with deference, and to the young suddenly giving a flash of her rare sweet smile.

As Lydia bowed and murmured and chatted to the Glovers' friends she made her way to Matthew. He was the centre of a group which comprised many business and professional acquaintances, the Vicar of St. Jude's from Warwick, and old Doctor Armstrong. The Misses Shelverdine, whose school on the Parade the girls had attended, hovered on the edge of the group as did dear dead Cissie's relations. Two of her pale dispirited sisters had come over from Stratford. They regarded Matthew with fright and only met infrequently.

The afternoon sped on winged feet, and all too soon the married couple were in the carriage, (Matthew's of course; a provincial vicar's stipend would not even run to the luxury of a pony) and on the way to their own home a short distance away. Their faces caught by the sun in the afternoon light were a study in tranquillity.

The supper party that night was a happy one. Cook had surpassed herself, determined that the Master should find no fault in the first meal provided under Charity's supervision. She was fond of the girl she called "the little quiet one," and was pleased to think she would be answerable to her in future and not to Miss Hope, who in her opinion was flighty. Amy, the parlour maid, under the watchful eye of Archer, waited at table efficiently. Candlelight flickered down the long table onto trays of rich food, and long-stemmed roses glowed among the silver.

At the head of the table sat Matthew, expanding and comfortable. He beamed with contentment and wine, even encouraging Cissie's two insignificant sisters in his sweeping benevolent glance. He smiled at Thomas, his eldest brother—a smaller, less polished edition of himself. Thomas had from his youth loved the land and had taken over the Yorkshire farm on his father's death. He and Matthew had little in common and met infrequently, but a pleasant bond of affection existed between the two.

Next to Matthew sat Charity, quietly composed. If she had any misgivings none showed in her face. She kept her eyes expertly on the table, attentive to their guests. She was grateful for Aunt Lydia's presence and infectious laugh, knowing she could be relied upon to keep up a flow of stimulating conversation.

Hope, her eyes like stars, was buoyant. Mercy, sitting opposite, noticed how frequently she glanced at the clock and her light voice rose more rapidly than usual as if in nervous excitement. When their eyes met an elaborate pantomime of sighs and meaningless gestures ensued. Puzzled, Mercy decided to ignore it and joined in the conversation around her.

"I am anxious to hear more about the great exhibition you all attended last year. Do tell me about it," her aunt was saying. "I was so sorry to miss it, but felt Faith's wedding to be of greater importance, and I really couldn't desert Charles for too long especially as he was leaving for India this Spring."

"It was beautiful, and so exciting. Papa took us on the steam train and we simply seemed to fly along."

"It was thick with smoke though, and not too comfortable," broke in Hope, wrinkling her nose.

"Yes. But the flowers in Hyde Park were wonderful and the great glass house was enormous. The trees were even left growing inside it, and in the central hall a crystal fountain played. There was so much to see that to describe everything would take hours."

"We brought home some very good catalogues which the girls shall show you later," said Matthew.

"I think London is wonderful," burst in Hope. "The shops are not to be believed. Papa allowed us five sovereigns each to spend and I couldn't decide for two days what to buy. Charity spent hers on some dry old books."

"Very sensible of you, my dear," murmured the Warwick vicar.

Matthew smiled benignly. "We all know you have rather frivolous tastes, Hope, but I noticed that Mercy made several notes of the better exhibits and had her sketch book to hand. I must admit the displays were delightful. It was a trip well worth making."

"The ivories from India would please you, Aunt Lydia. But I expect you will be seeing these things every day, soon," ended Hope wistfully.

"I suppose I shall. Well, I must send you all a large parcel at Christmas. But the exhibition must have been a great achievement for all concerned, and I do hope there will be some praise for Prince Albert. I understand his efforts were tireless. Perhaps the public will approve of him more generously now."

"It made a great deal of money," rumbled Dr. Armstrong, "one can only hope the proceeds are spent in a good and fitting manner."

"The Army badly needs reorganising and the

neglected Navy is practically useless," Matthew mused, "but I believe plans are already afoot for property in Kensington Gore. A little speculation there might be a good thing."

"I thought you were speculating in railways, Matthew. Have you changed your mind?" This question came from Uncle Tom.

Lydia felt the conversation was becoming decidedly businesslike.

"Now, Matthew, no speculations tonight. Let us talk of the coming summer. I want to hear what the girls have planned. Charity will, I know, be more or less occupied, but what of the others?"

"I hope the house won't take up all of Charity's time," answered Mercy. "We are going through the library together and have only progressed along the top shelf."

"*Reading* the books you mean?" gasped one of the ladies.

"Oh yes. There is so much to learn; it is no good picking at random. I love the poetry best, but Charity is interested in everything, even law and industrial life. She is anxious to learn more about conditions in the mines and factories, and child labour . . . in fact everything," she ended enthusiastically.

A stunned silence fell on the table and Mercy looked about her uncertainly. What had she said? Her father kept a most extensive library and none of them had been forbidden to enter or remove the books as far as she knew. Neither Faith nor Hope showed the slightest interest in learning beyond the bare essentials, but she and Charity were kindred spirits and Papa cared also for literature, for she found many new editions both technical and fictional by contemporary authors appearing regularly on the shelves.

As she looked puzzled at their guests her eye met the stony stare of her uncle from Nottingham and she realised, too late, his own wool factory in that city must employ the child labour she had just decried. Avoiding his gaze she turned to her father, but his enquiring looked was fixed on Charity speculatively.

"My daughter a blue stocking?" he queried half humorously. "I hardly think it seemly or necessary for young ladies to delve into such unsavoury things. By all means read the newest suitable literature, but I advise you to leave more serious matters to gentlemen."

The set of Charity's jaw spoke in opposition.

"But, Papa, such a lot goes on in the world, indeed in England alone, that is appalling and against all Christian practices. How many women of our station realise that children of five and six years old are working below ground in almost total darkness?"

Dr. Armstrong spoke. "The lower classes have to earn a living, my dear."

"Not in that way." Face flushed, the young girl spoke passionately. "Surely a living wage is the right of any man with a family to support."

"Ah, but where does the family stop?" asked Tom Glover.

"They need to be taught about these things, Uncle Tom."

The table was shocked to silence, looking

askance at this strange agitated girl in their midst. A well nurtured, sheltered young woman discussing such ugly details was disturbing and brought a gasp of horror from two of the ladies. Papa's brows met ominously.

"That is enough, Charity. I do not wish to forbid you access to my books but any further discussion on these lines will force me to do so. It is fortunate your thoughts will be too occupied in future with a more suitable subject."

Lydia caught her niece's eye. "Shall we leave the gentlemen to their wine, my dear?"

The colour had gone from Charity's face and she nodded composedly. She bowed slightly in an old-fashioned way to her father.

"Papa, we will adjourn to the drawing-room and prepare for some music later."

Mercy could not contain herself as the ladies proceeded upstairs.

"It was all my fault for talking too much. Papa would never have known your views if I'd been more discreet. I'm so sorry."

"It doesn't matter," came the unruffled reply. "I think I can handle Papa."

Lydia, after settling the other discreetly whispering ladies comfortably, came over to the girls. She was determined to pass over the scene as of little importance. She knew Matthew's bark was worse than his bite and he had to establish his authority in front of guests. She felt that beneath the anger he might well feel a certain pride that one member of his family had probably inherited his quite considerable brain. He had often talked with pride of his modern outlook, and the freedom his family were allowed, therefore he must take the consequences if his practices rebounded in an unorthodox way.

She went to the window and joined Hope, who was gazing into the twilight garden.

"It's a lovely night, the perfect end to a wonderful day."

Hope nodded. "I have a slight headache and I know Papa will expect me to sing. Do you think you could take my place, Aunt? You sing beautifully, and if I slip away now no one will miss me. I'll go straight to my room."

She left at once, assuring her aunt she would bathe her aching head with cologne.

The party broke up earlier than usual. Matthew was disappointed at Hope's early retirement. He missed her appearance enhancing the beauty of his drawing-room.

With his guests' departure he entered the library and sinking into a comfortable chair surveyed his handsome books appraisingly.

As his sister had silently predicted, the astonishment he felt at Charity's attitude was still on his mind. He tried to stifle the pride that would arise in him when he thought of her intelligent mind absorbing things so totally foreign to a woman's nature. What a pity she wasn't a boy. But there was still no excuse for her outspoken words. However much he might secretly admire her knowledge, she must behave as any normal young woman should in keeping with her station, and as keeper of his house.

THREE

ON THE VERY DAY of the wedding Hope had arranged to have Faith's room prepared for her own occupancy. She was, she declared, more than delighted to have some privacy, and had no intention of sharing any longer than necessary.

Mercy, when leaving the others on her way to bed, had peeped sympathetically into that room and was only slightly surprised to find the bed unoccupied and Hope missing. She had been suspicious all evening of her sister's behaviour and guessed something was afoot. Quite what she expected was uncertain, until the evidence of a letter scribbled in Hope's childish hand was discovered on her own pillow.

"Please come down and unlock the back staircase after Papa has gone to bed," it read. "Darling Mercy, be as quiet as a mouse."

It was now well after midnight. Three times Mercy had crept to the first landing and peeping through the banisters had, each time, seen a crack of light under the library door. How much longer would her father be before turning down the lamps and going to his room? She opened her door quietly once more, then shut it abruptly as candlelight flickered over the carpet below. Anxiously, ear pressed to the door she waited until the heavy tread passed. Archer might be hovering near her father's room, but the chances were that he had been excused his late duties after the long day, so once Papa's bedroom door was closed the coast would be clear. She waited another five minutes but all was still, so speeding stealthily down the back stairs she peered out into the night. With mist swirling from the river came a whisper of silk and suddenly Hope stepped in. Her face was radiant, with fair hair falling to her shoulders in abandon. She was shaking with relief.

"Thank goodness you're here," she said. "I've been waiting ages. Whatever kept you?"

"I couldn't come before; Papa's only just gone up and it's half past twelve. Where *have* you been? Your shawl is quite damp."

"I've been walking by the river in the moonlight with the most wonderful man in the world."

"Man. What man?"

"Harry Betteridge, of course, you goose."

In the safety of Hope's room the sisters faced each other.

"We arranged a meeting this afternoon and I thought supper would never end. It was agonising trying to get away by ten o'clock."

"Harry Betteridge? You mean Alfred's cousin from Oxford? But, Hope, you have only just met."

"I feel I have known him all my life, and have never met anyone like him before. He held my hand all the time we walked and he called me the most beautiful girl in the world."

Mercy, young and vulnerable, shared her sister's excitement. A lovers' tryst, a stolen meeting in the hush of night thrilled her, and in spite of her anxiety, a sympathy for the bright-eyed girl awoke.

"How long is he staying in town?"

"At least a week, and I've promised to meet him every night. He's going over to the vicarage tomorrow to call on Faith and I want to be near him whenever I can. There will be no gossip if you and I go together."

The practical side of Mercy's nature stifled her romanticism. "It seems very improper. What about Papa?"

"Oh, fiddlesticks to Papa. There is no need for him to be told, at least not yet. I don't want anyone to know."

"Not even Charity?"

"Certainly not Charity. She hasn't a romantic thought in her head and I am quite sure she will never get a husband if she carries on the way she did at supper tonight. Men don't want a woman whose mind is full of books and the everlasting poor. Harry says I listen beautifully and am soft and kittenish, just as a girl should be."

She paused and flung her arms around her sister's neck.

"Don't tell a soul, will you? I only confided in you because I want someone to share my happiness and I know you can be trusted to keep a secret."

Mercy smiled ruefully as she departed, but it

wasn't until the next day when she saw Hope and Harry together that the burden of the secret was brought home to her.

Faith, blushing with pleasure, welcomed her sisters to her home, offering cakes and tea in delicate china cups—a wedding present from Aunt Lydia.

When later Harry arrived unexpectedly there was some confusion on the bride's part, but Alfred entertained his cousin admirably.

Mercy felt the day was full of surprises. The warmth and love surrounding the newly married couple delighted her, but it failed to stop her covertly watching the handsome Harry Betteridge as he sat airily balancing a dainty cup on his knee. He certainly was very assured and suave, and she was disconcerted by the way his bold eyes indelicately sought out Hope's. The object of his attention fluttered and murmured and patted her becoming bonnet provocatively, fully aware of the impression she was making. Had not the bride and groom been so wrapped up in each other, Mercy felt that they could not have failed to notice this exhibition. They seemed so happy together starting their new life in this cold unpromising house Faith had, with colourful touches, done much to enlighten.

Mercy beamed as she hugged her sister on departure.

"I may come and visit you often, mayn't I?"

"Of course, you must both come. Perhaps before returning to Oxford we shall see you again, Harry also."

As the three of them crossed the park to Holly

Walk, Harry, walking between them, tucked both girls' hands under his arm. Mercy glanced at her sister who seemed about to swoon with delight, and she felt her own laughter bubbling to the surface as they bowed here and there to a scandalised acquaintance. Many a drawing-room that evening would be speculating on the stranger escorting Mr. Glover's two young daughters in so familiar a manner.

Before leaving them, Harry issued an invitation. "I would be delighted if you would both take tea with me. What about tomorrow?"

Hope blushed and nodded. "That would be very pleasant. Don't you agree, Mercy?"

Her sister looked at her aghast.

"We can't be seen in a hotel. Whatever would Papa say? He even disapproves when Aunt Lydia takes us to tea in the Pump Rooms."

"You are being foolish, Mercy."

Turning to the young man, Hope laughed in a tinkling artificial way. "My sister is very young; you must forgive her."

"I shall soon be seventeen," came the sharp reply. "And anyway we are going to Birmingham with Aunt Lydia tomorrow. You know it has been planned for days."

"Well, I am sure I can avoid the outing, so I shall certainly take tea with you, Harry."

The tall figure at her side swept off his hat and, when bidding them goodbye, bent low over Hope's hand whispering words Mercy failed to hear.

With heightened colour she followed Hope's

mincing steps towards home angrily guessing she was being used, and was convinced another clandestine meeting had been arranged over her head. She felt uneasy about her headstrong sister who was very susceptible to men with Harry Betteridge's looks and charm. Although she herself was younger by three years, she believed her own judgement of character and sensitivity to be far greater than Hope's. In spite of his overwhelming gaiety, an instinctive distrust of this persuasive man troubled her.

Glancing at the other's happy and determined face as they walked along, she said, "I do think you are being stupid. Word is sure to reach Papa."

"I hardly think so. People using the Regent Hotel are not Papa's friends. We shall arrange it most carefully, never fear."

That evening the weather changed and a steady downpour of rain fell continually from six o'clock. Hope was nervous and made endless trips to the window until Papa told her to sit down and stop fidgeting.

"The garden is exceedingly dry and the rain most welcome," he said. "But I've no doubt by tomorrow the skies will be clear again and your trip to Birmingham not delayed."

Shortly afterwards Hope retired to bed, complaining again of a throbbing headache.

"I feel you should call Dr. Armstrong if these pains persist," Lydia told her brother. "There must be a reason for them."

Mercy glanced up, guilt flooding over her. Only she understood the "sufferer's" motives. She was glad herself that the weather forbade another secret meeting. The deceits of tomorrow had yet to be discovered.

Matthew's optimism was well founded and the next day was bright and sunny. Lydia, Charity, and Mercy left early in their aunt's carriage, bound for the exciting emporiums of Birmingham.

They left Hope in her darkened room, assuring them she would shortly recover but insisting they enjoy the day without her. Only Mercy read the deception in her eyes and was almost tempted to confide in her more mature companions. To think that Hope, who loved shopping, was prepared to forgo such a treat for a casual acquaintance was disturbing indeed. However, she had given her word and perhaps she was being over-pessimistic. After all, they had only known the man a few days and by next week he would be gone.

Lydia Asterling had a delightful knack of doing everything in style and making any outing infinitely exciting. She discovered which shops were best to patronize and where to buy the most tantalizing bonnets, while Charity was allowed an hour in a musty old bookshop in the Bull Ring. The girls, filled with admiration at their aunt's calm assurance, realised it was her persuasive tongue that brought magic to each day.

The carriage turned into Holly Walk promptly at nine o'clock laden with parcels and gay banded boxes.

As they entered the house to an unusual silence, Charity glanced a little anxiously towards the kitchen quarters. Although she had organised everything in advance, she felt slightly guilty at leaving her duties all day.

Amy, coming out of the dining-room, was waylaid by Lydia.

"Wait a moment, Amy. Where is everyone? Has Miss Hope recovered from her headache?"

"Yes, my lady. Miss Hope is in her room."

"And where is Papa?" asked Charity.

"The Master is in the library, Miss. I was just putting the finishing touches to the table. Supper has been delayed as you wished. Shall I tell Cook you are back, Miss?"

"Yes please, Amy. We shall be ready in ten minutes."

Before they reached the staircase, however, Matthew's voice could be heard raised in an alarming manner.

"So you are back. Good. Come in girls please. I want a word with you. Will you be good enough to excuse us, Lydia?"

"Is there something wrong, Matthew? I would like to be present if I may. Surely I am allowed to share the family troubles."

"As you wish."

The apprehensive girls, their gay spirits deflated with unwelcome abruptness, entered the library.

"Did either of you know that Hope has been deceiving me by keeping secret assignations?" Matthew immediately barked at them.

Charity stared at her father unbelievingly, while a warm flush coloured Mercy's face. It passed unnoticed as Matthew continued explosively.

"It has been brought to my notice that a daughter of mine was seen taking refreshment at the Regent Hotel in the company of a . . . of a male person."

"But that's impossible," Charity cried.

"Not at all, my child. She seems to have regained her health with remarkable speed, and was decidedly well enough to laugh and joke in an unseemly manner at this afternoon's public tea party. And to think I entertained the fellow but a few days ago in my own house. I cannot say I cared very much for him then—extremely worldly for so young a man. I am inclined to think Faith was wrong to marry into a family with such unsavoury members."

"Calm down, Matthew, and tell us whom you are accusing." Lydia advanced towards her brother. "Quite possibly Hope saw no harm in the escapade; anyway there is nothing very dreadful about it, surely."

"Perhaps not to you, Lydia. With your wordly connections the life you lead is very different from that of a small provincial town. Kindly remember that I have a fair standing in the community and an episode like this can do a great deal to ruin the chances of good marriages for the girls. The reputation of Hope has, I fear, been very much impaired by this afternoon's events, and the despicable behaviour of this Betteridge fellow . . . Alfred's cousin in the bargain!"

Sympathetically Lydia agreed with her brother. But privately she thought he was being more than a little pompous and considering the damage to his own reputation more than that of the culprit. She could understand and justify his anger to some extent, realising what high hopes he had for his loveliest and favourite daughter. It was ineffectual to point out the deed's triviality. Matthew's world and that of his family centred round this narrow little town. She spoke quietly and soothingly to Matthew, sent the two girls off to dress, with a whispered message to bring Hope down to supper without fail.

The meal was a gloomy affair. Matthew sat stiffly at the table, glowering every time he glanced at the fair head of his offending daughter. He was upset and puzzled by her. The floods of repentant tears he expected failed to flow; therefore he was not prepared to be reasonable. Hope sat, with remarkably dry eyes and a glitter of defiance in their depths, her cheeks pink with frustration. No apology was forthcoming he noticed irritably and felt the flouting of his authority insufferable. Her rebellion must be firmly quelled.

He waited until the meal was over, then, as Charity rose, motioned to her to remain seated.

"Wait. Kindly sit down. You too, Lydia, if you insist on sharing our quarrels. I have a few remarks to make and I wish for your undivided attention."

As they all meekly subsided he looked searchingly at each of his daughters until his eyes finally rested on Hope.

"Much as it distresses me I do not wish to dwell on Hope's disgraceful conduct but certainly I am reconsidering the licence I allow you. Never have I refused any reasonable request. You are able to walk where you will, visiting town and gardens and many public places unchaperoned; outings that I am sure many of your friends are denied. Now for a while your freedom must be curtailed, so I shall forbid any of you to venture out of the house for at least one week."

A silence followed. Hope stifled a gasp of dismay, and Charity made no reply. Mercy was appalled.

"But, Papa," she cried, "what about Gyp? Who will take him for his walk?"

"I will see that Jim exercises your dog for a few days, my dear. I am sorry that you all have to suffer the consequences of another's bad behaviour. By doing this I trust that Hope's conscience will prevent her from repeating any further indiscretions."

Lydia interrupted him.

"Do try to remember, Matthew, the girls are no longer children and you cannot resort to schoolroom tactics at their age. You expect them to take over certain responsibilities, therefore you must treat them as adults. I am not denying it was wrong of Hope to deceive you, but the last few weeks have been distracting to say the least." She had been studying the rebellious face of the culprit and suddenly made a decision.

"I think a little change would be good for all of them. You know, Matthew, that I intend going to London within the next few days; certain domestic matters oblige me to extend my stay in England for a while. I think I shall open our house at Richmond and I feel it might be a good idea to take two of the girls with me."

Matthew spoke after reflection.

"That might indeed be the answer. It is Charity's duty to look after the house, but we must be fair. I think they should all go."

"Oh, no," burst in Hope swiftly, "let me stay behind. It should be my punishment."

A brighter look came over Matthew's face and he bestowed a kindlier look on the speaker.

Before he could reply, however, Mercy cried in a surprised voice, "But you adore London. You said only the other day. . . ."

"Be quiet," snapped Hope. "Why should Charity be penalised for me? And you know, Papa, how you would hate the silent house without at least one of us here for company."

Charity's soft voice spoke from the head of the table.

"In spite of Papa's kind thought I agree with Hope and really feel he would be very lonely with all of us gone. You know how little I care for London; and I have all those books I bought today that I am simply longing to read. I am quite content to stay at home and, in fact, would welcome the peace. I will look after Gyp for you, Mercy."

The younger girl beamed at Charity, a smile replacing the troubled frown.

"Well, if you are sure. Oh, it will be lovely. When shall we be leaving?"

A laugh of relief rippled round the table at the girl's eagerness and the happier turn of events.

"I think Friday will be ideal if it can be arranged."

"But that's the day after tomorrow." Hope became agitated. "Must it be so soon?" She averted her eyes but with faltering voice continued. "I'll never be ready. My clothes need organising and. . . ."

"Nonsense," Matthew broke in briskly. "There is no need to worry about your wardrobe. I shall provide you all with enough money to purchase several gowns and any other articles you may require. Is there anything further you wish to add?"

Seeing his watchful eyes scrutinising her, the look of defiance faded from the girl's face. "No, Papa."

As they rose from the table, the finality in Matthew's voice forbade any further discussion.

"It is settled then. Thank you for your kind offer, Lydia. On Friday, Mercy and Hope will go with you to London."

Later, Mercy followed a furious Hope to her room. She found her sister on the bed, eyes blazing, her face hostile.

"I won't go," she stormed. "He can't make me. I've got to see Harry again; he goes back to Oxford on Monday. Oh, why can't the trip be postponed until then?"

"Simply because Papa suspects you are planning something," Mercy replied sagely. "Whatever happened this afternoon?"

"Miss Shelverdine saw us through the tea-room window. I can't think how she got to Papa so fast. She must have simply flown down the Parade. He was waiting for me when I got home."

"Was he very angry?"

"Enough, as you could see for yourself. I thought I could talk him round, but somehow whatever I said failed to pacify him. We knew there would be trouble so Harry waited, but Papa of course refused to see him. I've just got to meet him again, Mercy, and go tonight as planned. You must help me."

"I think you are taking too many chances. If Papa finds out you are still deceiving him he might send you to Uncle Tom in Yorkshire. Think how you would hate that, on the moors far away from everyone. Please don't upset him further."

Hope bit her nail. "But what shall I do without Harry? I love him, Mercy, and he loves me. He has promised to write to me every day and when he's finished his studies is coming back to marry me."

Mercy was aghast. "I am sure Papa will never give his consent, and anyway you hardly know him."

"Love doesn't waste time as you will understand when you are older. Do you realise if I go to London with you, Harry and I will only have tonight and tomorrow." She broke off, suddenly alert. "Isn't tonight Papa's meeting at the Assembly Hall? Well, I am going to meet Harry as arranged. Don't worry, I'll be very careful. I've no intention of making things more difficult for myself. I shall be back at the usual time, so remember to open the door for me. When Harry and I are happily married I shall look back and remember your help and how you made these wonderful meetings possible."

FOUR

THE TRIP TO Richmond was a great success, their stay of two weeks a continual bustle of activity.

Hope, meekly submitting to her father's wishes, had left Holly Walk with her aunt and Mercy in a mild contrite manner. Both her companions were wary of this sudden capitulation and Lydia vowed to keep a sharp eye on the culprit.

They had been away but three days however, when letters began to arrive. Hope made no secret of the fact they were from Harry, and Lydia saw no harm in allowing the girl this concession. In her opinion furtiveness was unhealthy and the more openly things were discussed and naturally accepted, the sooner the affair would die.

In spite of what she considered the harsh treatment of her father, and although she admitted to answering Harry's letters daily, Hope's supposedly undying love failed to prevent her from enjoying to the full the gaiety of London.

The new friends of both sexes they made brought equal delight to the girls. Shopping, followed by the ballet or opera made each day an adventure, and once their aunt allowed them an evening out with two young men ... of impeccable character of course. Visiting a music hall amused and exhilarated them and a warning to keep it secret from Papa led them to believe how gay and wicked and modern they had become.

They left for home gloomily. Life in the Midlands would seem very dull after the enchantment of the bustling cosmopolitan city.

"I don't know what to do about Harry's letters once we arrive home," Hope worriedly remarked during the journey.

Lydia was disturbed. She had hoped the effects of their holiday would have dimmed the bloom of this first young love.

"Perhaps it would be a good idea to gradually discontinue the correspondence," she suggested tactfully.

"Oh no, not that. Because I have been cheerful you may think I have forgotten Harry, but I assure you I have not," she answered emphatically. "His letters are exquisite and I cannot live without them."

Lydia sighed. It seemed that nothing would prevent the affair from flourishing. She had done her best; now it was for Matthew to come to terms with Hope's waywardness.

Mercy's sympathetic nature when later the sisters were alone tempted her to offer some comfort.

"Perhaps Papa will have cooled down and may allow you to correspond."

"I am quite sure he won't. I suspect he has someone already in mind for me to marry. Sir William Weston's son is looking for a bride and although he is really quite old the prestige of a title and that crumbling old place near Kenilworth would, I am sure, suit Papa nicely," Hope answered spitefully.

"Oh no, be fair. He would never force you into an unhappy marriage; he loves you too much for that."

"That's as may be." Hope felt slightly ashamed of herself, but throwing off the mood, reflectively continued: "I wonder if Faith would receive Harry's letters for me."

"Certainly not. How can you involve her in such a deceitful plan? Besides, Alfred would instantly forbid it."

"Yes. I suppose you are right. Although I shall be quite desperate if I don't think of something soon."

Both Charity and Matthew received them home with pleasure. The warm kiss her father bestowed on Hope told her all was forgiven. He listened indulgently to the details of every outing. The eyes of Hope and Mercy met in secret merriment as they omitted a few of the gayer events.

The ban of house confinement was now of course abolished, and June and July sped on golden wings. Hope seemed to have gotten over her infatuation for that unsuitable young man. He had left the district and his name was carefully avoided. Matthew had lectured Alfred on his undesirable cousin, advising him to discourage further visits to the Midlands in the future. Although puzzled over this, Alfred had assumed there was some logical explanation. He wasn't particularly fond of Harry himself, considering him far too worldly and irresponsible for the serious business of life. Alfred had problems of his own with so large a parish to attend. Many miles were tramped during the sultry weather giving succour, advice, and not a little medical aid to his poor but faithful parishioners. He was happy to return in the evening to the cool vicarage garden where Faith, now in early pregnancy, was waiting, excellent housewife that she was, with a supper he considered worthy of a king.

When in August Lydia made plans to sail to India the girls were dejected. The gaiety of their aunt's presence and the loving care she had lavished on them during her four months' stay would be sadly missed.

Matthew thought with regret of her faint perfume, and the absent whispering silk of her gowns would be deplored. Her practical knowledge had been invaluable, too, particularly during that distasteful affair in June which had caused him to scrutinise Hope's character with distinct unease. He was blissfully ignorant of the fact that his incorrigible daughter was still keeping up a smouldering correspondence with Harry Betteridge.

The manager of the Regent Hotel had not seen fit to report to her father that Hope Glover was regularly the recipient of letters collected by Jim, that gentleman's own stable lad, on his jaunts into town three times a week. After all he was paid to keep his own counsel and the sovereigns slipped discreetly into his hand occasionally by the young lady in question were more than welcome.

Charity, serenely working in a world of her own among the domestic chores, was totally ignorant of her sister's deception and even Mercy, knowing Hope as she did, believed the affair was over.

The morning Lydia departed was wet. Rain fell heavily from daybreak, the dripping trees mingling with their tears as the girls waved their goodbyes. Lydia's eyes too were wet as she leaned out of the carriage.

"Come, girls," she cried. "Let me see you smile; it won't be for ever you know. A few years will bring me back, to other weddings no doubt. Goodbye, goodbye."

Gyp came bounding up wet and bedraggled and Mercy knelt to hug him, hiding her tear-stained face in his coat. Charity caught her hand and the collar of Gyp and together they entered the quiet house.

Hope had already run upstairs, her wide shirts swinging about her pretty legs. There had been something odd about Hope these last few days: she seemed to quiver with suppressed excitement. Mercy, alert and observant, felt she was glad of the bustle of their aunt's departure as if anxious to draw attention from herself. What ulterior motive was behind her actions? The thought crossed her mind that Harry Betteridge might again be on the scene. She knew the University was on summer vacation but surely he would never dare try to renew his acquaintance with her sister.

She took Gyp to the kitchen for a cleanup and as she went upstairs the front door slammed.

Charity stood on the top landing, startled.

"I thought I heard you going out," she called.

"It's raining far too hard at present," Mercy answered. "It may have been the wind."

"Perhaps. I am looking for Hope. Do you know where she is?"

"She must be about somewhere; this is not the weather to take her out unless she's gone over to the Vicarage."

"Hardly likely I think. Alfred is nursing a cold and Hope is not fond of him at the best of times."

As she entered her room the letter seemed to rise and hit Mercy in the face. She opened it with trembling fingers, calling for Charity in fright.

Together they read it, stark in its simplicity.

"I HAVE GONE AWAY WITH HARRY. PLEASE FORGIVE ME, DARLING MERCY, AND EXPLAIN TO PAPA. I LOVE YOU ALL, BUT I LOVE HARRY BEST.
        HOPE."

FIVE

ALTHOUGH THE SUN continued to shine constantly that summer, a gloom settled over the house in Holly Walk. Laughter was absent for many a long day, and even Gyp's barking subdued, as if he too sensed the depression.

It seemed to Mercy to go on for ever and although her good sense told her it must be only weeks before things were more or less back to normal, they would never really be *quite* the same again. How would they ever forget that dreary damp day when, with the departure of Aunt Lydia, Hope had left the house forever.

Silently, the sisters had waited all day, refusing the food Cook sent them, sick with anxiety for their father's return. Charity had broken the news to him in her own quiet way, voice firm and compassionate. Only the chalk-white face and tightly clasped hands betrayed her nervousness. The girls would never forget the look in his eyes as the truth sank in.

Rage, incredulity, the usual quick flash of temper, anything would have been more characteristic than the complete silence with which he received the stunning blow. For a few moments his eyes dilated, then sank, sombre, back into his head.

"Thank you for telling me."

His voice was scarcely audible as he spoke and withdrawing into the library he closed the door firmly behind him.

How many hours he was there they never knew, but the next morning he arrived at breakfast, calm and immaculate as ever. Meals in this house had always been lively affairs. The girls had never been discouraged even as children to talk at the table as was the usual custom. The deep silence this morning therefore was foreign, but he seemed oblivious of it and read the *Courier* in his usual way. He folded his napkin meticulously at the end of the meal, rang for Archer and gave instructions to have his carriage delayed, then turned to face his daughters. Seriously he looked at them with frowning calculation before speaking.

"It seems with the departure of your Aunt Lydia there is another absent place at our table, one which can never again be filled. I have very little to say to you except that I feel you are both equally blameless in this affair. I cannot believe that had either of you known of such underhand practices you would have kept me in ignorance. That a daughter of mine could behave with such deception is beyond my understanding." He paused to control the tremor in his voice. "In fact I no longer consider Hope my daughter and therefore from this day I forbid the mention of her name in my house in any circumstances. Do I make myself clear?"

"Oh, Papa." The strain of the last few hours caused Mercy to burst into passionate weeping.

"Calm yourself, my dear. My decision may seem harsh to you but I believe in the interests of all concerned I am adopting the best policy. I should advise you to get away into your beloved fields for a few hours," her father continued kindly. "The weather has improved and it is a beautiful day. When I return this evening I shall expect everything to be as normal as possible. I will deal with the kitchen staff myself. Charity, you will, I am sure, have more than enough to occupy you. Inform your sister Faith as you think fit, bearing in mind naturally her present condition."

He rose and going to each girl lightly kissed the top of their heads without emotion.

Mercy fled to the outside world for comfort, frightened at the unknown quantity in her father, yet realising how bitter was his hurt. She felt suddenly very young and helpless and acutely aware of the gulf between them. Never had he seemed so remote and unapproachable. When harmony prevailed the family seemed closely-knit and happy. Surely then, when grief and misery was rife, they should not be left to mourn alone. There should be a bridge to tread the troubled waters together.

Charity, brooding silently, proceeded with her work. What explanation her father had given below stairs she was unaware, but Cook treated her with unusual civility and Archer went out of his way to please.

THE HOUSE IN HOLLY WALK

With her usual calm, Faith received the news. Now that she was no longer a member of her father's household she felt a guilty reluctance to be involved in the crisis. She was naturally distressed but Alfred's stability helped her view things with a curious detachment. Alfred, hiding his agitation, was as staunch as a rock. Inwardly he grieved at the thought of a member of his own family creating such havoc among his wife's relations. He took Charity's little hands in his own large reassuring ones, offering hospitality and spiritual guidance to herself and Mercy whenever they felt the need.

"How do we treat our friends and relatives?" Faith asked. "They are sure to make enquiries."

"We are to inform people that she is away visiting. Papa insists that nothing more is necessary at present. It will be very difficult."

Indeed it was difficult. In the following weeks the town buzzed with gossip and speculation. The mysterious disappearance of Mr. Glover's daughter was the primary topic in every lady's drawing-room.

Almost three weeks later a letter arrived for Mercy. The pale blue envelope addressed in Hope's handwriting lay with the other post beside her father's plate. She sat waiting in an agony of anticipation for Matthew to appear; to take it up without permission was unheard of.

When their father appeared, he smiled and methodically started sorting his mail. Picking up the blue envelope thoughtfully and without comment he swiftly and deliberately tore the letter unopened into a dozen pieces. The tiny white lines on either side of his nose told the elder girl what it cost him to do this, and the rigid grip of his hands belied his indifference.

Mercy could scarcely believe her eyes. She gasped in anguish and disappointment, and rushed in angrily.

"Papa, that was *my* letter."

"Nothing of importance I am sure, my dear." He frowned. "I dislike your tone, Mercy; kindly continue your breakfast."

Later she stormed rebelliously to her sister.

"How can he be so heartless and cruel? Where do you think the letter came from? I didn't get a chance to see the postmark, but I'm sure it was a foreign stamp."

"I have asked Alfred to discover what he can of his cousin's plans. We know he has another year at Oxford so unless he abandons his studies that's where he's likely to be, and probably Hope too."

The frustration of waiting for news became increasingly worrying. Mercy found their father more difficult to understand than Charity did. She longed to share some of his unhappiness, but his withdrawal from them during the past weeks had sown a certain timidity in her.

Charity's naturally undemonstrative nature shrank too from approaching him. Although her father had invariably been as considerate to her as the others, she always found it difficult to show her affection for him and had held herself aloof. With her continuous reading she found herself viewing men with the lowest esteem. Admiring her father for his good qualities, this did nothing to alter her opinion of his sex, and she felt a strong compunction towards them. The women of the world, particularly the poorer classes, led a joyless life to her way of thinking. Continually bearing children, fighting to make ends meet, burdened with a husband ill able to provide on his pitiful wages, what chance did such a woman have to develop a life of her own? The cycle went drearily on, day after day, until all was finished and death was welcomed, often too soon. Was this what life was for? Were women born to be used by men? To serve no other purpose than a chattel, prized lower than the animals on the farms? At least the animals could be sold in market when their useful days were done.

How often Charity would ponder, far into the night, chafing at her inability to help, longing to break away and lead a more rewarding life. She helped with church work and administered to the poor of the parish. But here, in this flourishing little town dire poverty was comparatively unknown. She read so much of London, Glasgow and Wales, where hungry mouths cried out for food, and frustration caused her much heart-searching and hours of untold pain. She took an interest in several needy local families. Her gentle hands, providing and administering medical aids, repeatedly relieved the pains of many an ailing mother. These worn, harassed, overworked women spoke so highly of her that the perplexed staff at Holly Walk hardly knew what to make of their young mistress. She had always appeared aloof to them, pleasant enough maybe, but lacking the open friendliness of the other girls.

Mercy continued to fret, and spent hours after their father had departed awaiting delivery of the second mail. One or two further blue envelopes were fleetingly glimpsed by Charity, but she wisely kept this knowledge to herself. Later, they either ceased altogether or were, she presumed, quickly disposed of.

With the advent of Christmas, entertaining was revived. The house hung gay with festoons, holly and evergreens, and for the first time the new German custom of a tall trimmed fir tree stood gaily decorating the candelit hall.

Friends and relatives were gratified to attend parties at Matthew's house, where no expense was spared for the comfort of his guests.

Christmas seemed as other years had been except that Faith, heavily pregnant, was spared the activity of previous ones, and the absence of a bright golden head under a flutter of gay ribbons, silently regretted. The forbidden name was not even whispered, and only Charity noticed her father's shadowed eyes and the lack of Mercy's spontaneous laughter.

A large parcel arrived from overseas full of beautiful Indian silks, glossy shawls and native crafts. Lydia enclosed a letter giving them news of the exotic East, and disturbing tales of the unrest out there. It was obvious she had not as yet received Charity's letter conveying their own lamentable news, for there was an unclaimed parcel Mercy tactfully whisked away from her father's eyes and hid unopened in her own room. She was convinced the day would come when Hope would herself claim it.

On a wet, cold February night Faith's daughter was born. Mercy and Charity were delighted with the tiny red-faced scrap of humanity. Matthew, if disappointed that his first grandchild was female, failed to show it. He went over to the vicarage personally, bearing generous gifts, and invited a few friends that evening to wet the baby's head.

It seemed no time at all before Mercy, acting as nursemaid, was wheeling her niece in the public gardens. She was thinking of last spring and her sister's wedding. What changes had taken place since then!

There had been no further word from Hope. Where was she, and what had happened to her in her nine months' absence? Alfred's discovery that Harry was travelling Europe—a luxury provided by his grandfather's will—could only mean that Hope, now being his wife, was accompanying him. The two girls at home through the cold English winter envied the sunshine and pleasure she must be enjoying.

Gently rocking the baby backwards and forwards, Mercy, her book lying idly on her lap, was oblivious of nodding acquaintances as she sat by the lake. She was not at the moment thinking of Hope but was more concerned with Charity. Of late her sister had drawn into a world of her own, shutting herself away in her room whenever she could escape from her tasks, writing letters it seemed by the score. So often was there correspondence for her that Papa had remarked on it more than once, looking questioningly, but getting no response. What she wrote, and to whom, Charity was certainly not revealing, and although it brought an air of unrest it was her own secret matter.

Mercy, puzzled, was musing so deeply she failed to notice the baby carriage sliding gently towards the lake until almost the last moment.

Horrified, jumping to her feet, she saw a strong arm shoot in front of her and check carriage and baby abruptly.

"Oh goodness," she gasped, fright and relief mingling to set her heart beating rapidly. She looked up at the towering figure of a red-coated Army officer as he turned the perambulator towards her.

"Your baby, Madam, I think," he smiled, touching his hat smartly.

"Oh dear." Mercy, covered with confusion felt her cheeks burning with shame.

"I can't thank you enough. My sister would never have forgiven me if anything had happened to her little girl."

The officer bowed.

"Think nothing of it." He bent to recover her fallen book from the grass. "I see you are reading *David Copperfield*—Dickens' newest book, I believe. I do hope you are enjoying it."

"Yes, indeed," Mercy nodded. "Perhaps you have read it, too?"

"Not yet. It takes a little time for new works to reach the far east."

"The far east? Where are you from, may I ask?"

"India. Delhi to be exact. I have three months' leave."

"But you are not a local man I am sure. I don't remember seeing you in the district."

"I am spending a few days here with the intention of finding relatives of friends in my regiment. I am a complete stranger to the Midlands, so perhaps you can oblige."

"By all means." Mercy beamed at him and he noticed with pleasure the chestnut curls peeping from beneath her green bonnet.

"My name is Mercy Glover, and I am sure I can help you, I know most people of note in the town."

"Glover?" The young man looked at her disbelievingly. "Did you say Glover? How extraordinary. There can't be more than one family of that name here. Do you live in Holly Walk?"

At Mercy's nod he laughed. "Then I need look no further. I have heard all about you and your family from your aunt, Lady Asterling. It is on her behalf I am looking up her brother and nieces."

Mercy felt so happy she could have thrown her arms around his neck.

"Aunt Lydia. How wonderful, I just can't believe it. How is she, and Uncle Charles?"

"Very well indeed. Sir Charles is my commanding officer but apart from this, both he and Lady Lydia I count among my closest friends. I have letters for all of you, and messages for your father."

"Papa will be delighted to see you. Both he and Charity will shortly be home. I have to return Cissie to the vicarage where you can meet my other sister. Then we will go straight to Holly Walk."

As they walked along she cast covert glances at the tall figure at her side. The lavish gold braid on his short jacket flashed in the sun and his jaunty shako tilted provocatively at her.

He told her his name was Miles Finch, Captain in the Gloucester Hussars. He walked with the rhythm of a true soldier, taking long effortless strides and his bronzed face leaned towards her, the dark eyes flashing where the ready humour lurked. Mercy felt an immense and curious pride as they left the park together.

Papa was genuinely pleased to welcome the young officer. At supper they encouraged him to talk of the East and expand on Lydia's life in that unknown country.

When learning his journey to the Midlands was especially to see them, Matthew insisted he remove his luggage immediately from the Regent Hotel and take up residence for the duration of his stay in Holly Walk.

To say the few days of his intention spread to weeks showed the instant attraction Matthew felt towards the young man. He found the stimulating intelligent, decidedly male, company a pleasant change from perpetual petticoats. Very soon Miles' natural ease and charm captivated them all.

Miles treated Matthew with more friendliness and familiarity than his own father would have allowed. They discussed many topical subjects, including the delicate situation of Hindu and Moslem serving with the British soldier abroad.

THE HOUSE IN HOLLY WALK

The likelihood of violence exploding only too soon in secretive restless India was disquieting. They discussed the British Government, agreed on its extravagances and inadequate rule, and generally together put the world to rights.

Matthew was delighted with him, his tall military bearing, dark good looks, and quick wit and humour. Not wishing to pry into the young man's affairs, he found the casual way Miles mentioned his family and background without restraint revealed a frank and open nature. His father was a well known influential figure of good connections, with a country seat in Gloucestershire and a house in town. Miles might simply be a second son, but his financial future was secure, and Matthew's calculating head already saw him as a prospective son-in-law.

It was a pity about Hope of course. How often unwillingly he would think with longing of his golden-haired darling, only to suppress such treacherous thoughts stonily, but furtively he matched her with Miles. She, so fair and lovely, he so dark and debonair. A perfect complement for each other.

Miles treated both girls with equal gallantry and candour, assisting Charity on her bounteous errands, carrying her laden basket and often helping with odious tasks. He sought out books for her delight and new pens or writing materials whenever he ventured into the nearby towns. Charity accepted it all gratefully with her slow sweet smile but never quite acknowledging the grace of the young man's presence.

With Mercy he was charming. He accompanied her and Gyp on long country walks. They would carry a picnic basket and disappear for long hours. Matthew wondered about Mercy, returning from their jaunts hung with daisy chains, her bonnet swinging by its ribbons, face aglow, auburn curls flying. They seemed ideally suited but was she too young? What did they talk about during those long golden days? Did Miles look upon her as he might a pretty young sister?

Matthew would have given much for his sister Lydia's sound advice. The unbiased opinion of a close friend would also be welcome, but he had no such friend and as the years went on he felt the deficiency keenly and regretted his own aloofness.

To confide in Faith was unthinkable; she was too impassive and shy. Once again in early pregnancy, her own affairs naturally were of primary concern.

Frequently he considered Charity as she flitted about the house, serenely engrossed in her own thoughts. What went on in that secretive head was a mystery to him. He felt no communication with her at all, and yet he had the uncomfortable feeling that one day she might very well explode a bombshell in their midst.

That Miles Finch looked upon Mercy as a younger sister may have seemed likely to anyone but himself. There were three girls in his own family and the feeling he had for Mercy, although starting with sisterly casualness, was, he was well aware, rapidly growing into something stronger. He found her enchanting. She had more gaiety and less inhibitions than any other girl he knew. His own sisters led an extremely sheltered life in Gloucestershire, their own manners being lessons in decorum. Whenever in company no excited chatter or burst of impulsive laughter was heard, and any spontaneous smiles were hidden by elaborate fans. The restrictions he knew awaited him at home kept him lingering longer than he had intended in this sleepy provincial town.

Five years in the Queen's army had naturally not left him inexperienced, but whatever contacts with the opposite sex he had encountered were but light, passing pleasures.

Now, as he watched Mercy, natural, joyous, perhaps over-young, he knew that very soon his heart would be completely won. It was too early to take her to India. Protocol abroad was very exacting and never for a moment was a white woman left unattended. He thought of her, tender, untried, thrown into that select smothering society. Even the presence of her Aunt Lydia would do little to protect her. Chafe as he might, he knew the only thing to do was wait. His next leave would not be for five years. Could he expect her to wait that long? Five years—it seemed like eternity. But knowing the explosive situation in India and fully aware how swiftly tragedies occur, he could not be responsible for taking her, so inexperienced, into the dangerous unknown.

So, the summer idyll went on. The days spent alone with her were Heaven indeed. He admired the girl's sketchbook and encouraged her to paint unusual ferns and toadstools, drawing attention to much beautiful flora that had missed her eye. She would often, in fun, draw ridiculous little stick men until long strips of cartoons flowed from her pencil. Nests being built, and the flutter of wings in a hedge found them peeping at many fledgling.

Once they freed a rabbit from a snare and Miles was forced to kill the badly injured animal. Mercy wept copious tears and he tenderly took her in his arms until the sobbing subsided. As she moved and blew her nose on his handkerchief he felt himself trembling.

One day they were caught in a torrential thunderstorm and Miles had to carry her over an old stone bridge, awash from the swollen river. They collapsed on the far bank, drenched, to see a rainbow curving in a glow of light against the black sky. Mercy's eyes sparkled.

"Oh isn't it beautiful?" she breathed.

He looked at her, the rapid heartbeats thundering against his wet shirt. Looked at the glistening chestnut hair, at the wet shining lips and he bent his head swiftly and kissed her, fiercely, unrelentingly, until she gasped beneath his fervour. She clung to him rapturously and he held her until all trembling ceased, murmuring over and over, "Oh Mercy. Oh Mercy."

It took tremendous will power to release her and he saw she was shivering. He controlled his voice and pulled her to her feet.

"Come on, you'll get pneumonia. I'll race you to the edge of the wood."

She looked at him uncertainly and suddenly her radiant smile flashed out.

"All right, straight for home. After all, there's always tomorrow."

The tomorrow drifted into another week and then Miles made plans to leave.

There were endless messages to be delivered to Aunt Lydia and he himself promised to write both girls regularly.

To Mercy, he secretly gave a leather bound volume of Tennyson's poems, small enough for her to carry in her pocket. That there were marked passages for no other eyes but hers she was to discover when reading it later.

Everyone was sorry to see him go. Matthew, a sadness in his heart, stood with Charity by his side, urging a return visit as soon as further leave was permitted. The dark, unfathomable eyes of Charity rested on him with affection.

Mercy stood a little apart. Unshed tears made her eyes overbright and her lower lip trembled as she hushed Gyp's excited whimpering. Miles came over to her and took both her hands in his. He bent low and kissed her hot cheek, and his voice was for her alone, low and gentle.

"Goodbye, my darling Mercy. I shall come back to you one day if you will wait for me."

"Oh Miles," the girl was breathless. "I'll wait for ever."

She turned and ran up the wide staircase. Sobbing, she flung herself on the bed. It was her first taste of love, exquisite, agonising, unknown. Unsaid words stood between them like a barrier and would remain so until the day he returned, when he would break it down by claiming her for ever.

SIX

With neat, brown head bent low over the small desk, Charity, her short-sighted eyes screwed up with concentration, was absorbed in writing. Her father had insisted on Dr. Armstrong supplying her with spectacles, and she fidgeted with the small ill-fitting steel frames impatiently. She wore them when engaged in close work to please Papa, but knowing how she could manage equally well without them as long as her nose was almost resting on the print she secretly discarded them on many occasions.

She kept the lamp as low as possible for it was late, and for hours the house had been in darkness. Propped before her was a letter she had repeatedly read. It was from the Christian Socialist Movement offering her work ... or, more accurately, begging for her aid in their fight against squalor and hardship in London's East End. It was only one of the many letters she had lately received and each denomination was desperate for willing hands to help ease their insupportable burdens.

DOROTHY WAKELEY

She had put off too long facing Papa with her intentions. What would he say when she told him of her desire to go to London and work in the slums with these dedicated people. For months a burning ambition within her had grown and an ardent correspondence between herself and a few staunch social workers had fired it further. With this letter of encouragement in her hand she now felt able to face Papa. She knew without doubt the outraged incredulity he would show at the step she wished to take. His first objection would be her health, and she realised it would take all her powers of persuasion to convince him that in spite of her frail appearance she was fundamentally perfectly well.

She felt no guilt at leaving her present responsibilities. Mercy was now over eighteen and perfectly capable of looking after herself and her father.

Of Hope, nothing further had been heard, and although she and Mercy, unknown to their father had made several attempts to trace her, it had been to no avail.

A cold wind whistled across the garden bringing November mists up from the river. Listening, Charity heard a whimper of welcome from Gyp, while his tail thumped downstairs on the floor. Someone was still about. She saw the hands of her clock stood at ten minutes past one. She knew Papa slept badly. She had heard his steps many times in the silent hours and she guessed how his heart sorrowed, perhaps with regret. Though none must mention the forbidden name, both she and Mercy sensed the desolation in the heart of the proud unhappy man who was their father.

Suddenly a sharp knock on the door interrupted her thoughts, and her father stood there. He came forward, closing the door behind him.

"You are working very late, my dear," he said concernedly.

"I'm sorry, Papa, I have so much on my mind. If I go to bed I cannot sleep." She paused for a moment, then impulsively went on. Now was the time, while they were alone without fear of interruption.

"I know it is late, but could you spare me a little time, Papa? There is something of importance I would like to discuss with you."

"At this time of night. Surely it can wait until morning."

"I think not. When I tell you what I have in mind, I want you to hear me out to the end. Please bear with me, and promise not to interrupt until I have finished."

Her father sighed, but seated himself opposite her studying the lamplight on her face. God in Heaven, how like her mother she had grown, so small, so frail. The heavy shadowed eyes in the little pinched face looked about to burn themselves out. He nodded to her to continue, and when she spoke, her voice though low was firm and resolute.

"I want to go to London, Papa ... no wait, don't answer yet. I have been corresponding for over a year with friends of various charitable organisations. It is my ambition to share the burdens borne by these wonderful people and work in the East End with them. There is indescribable poverty there, and hardship which only a human presence can relieve. I want to administer to these unhappy creatures, to share their misery and pain."

Her father was astounded, and, biting back his first reaction of irritability, spoke reasonably.

"What good could you possibly do, you whose health is so indifferent? These social workers must be as strong and healthy as cattle, ready to face all odds. Things are very different in reality to pictures painted with words."

He flicked the papers on her desk disparagingly. "How could a young, inexperienced girl like yourself deal with drink and violence and vice? Things that you in your ignorance could never comprehend. It is a preposterous idea."

"I would learn, and I am not as ignorant as you imagine. I have been well supplied with literature and pamphlets written on life under appalling conditions.

"I have here an inspiring letter from a Miss Nightingale. She seems interested in my medical activities and treatment of the sick. I would like your comments on her letter please, Papa. She has been studying nursing methods in Germany and seems very self-assured."

"And what of your work here? What of the poor families here you have taken under your wing? Are they to starve of neglect while you go chasing off to London among your alien friends?"

"I have considered that. Mercy has been well schooled to assist where necessary. She has far more sense than you give her credit for. You need not worry for your own comfort either; that will not suffer I assure you."

Matthew felt annoyance rising in him again and he spoke sharply.

"My own welfare is of the least concern as I think you very well know and I do not underestimate your sister in the slightest. I do feel however that in spite of your concern for these deplorable wretches, a little thought should have gone into the condition of this already depleted house."

"The depletion is not strictly necessary," the girl flashed out. "You could find Hope and bring her home." She stopped, a horrified tremor in her voice as she tried to see her father's face in the gloom. Only the busy ticking of the clock broke the pregnant silence.

At last the man stirred. He passed his hands tiredly over his face as he rose from the chair.

"I shall erase that remark as unworthy of you, Charity. My feelings on that have been made more than plain. As for your own matters, I cannot bring myself to dwell on them fairly at this hour. You must realise what a shock your proposals are, and at present I feel there is a little hope of my falling in with your wishes. I shall indeed need time to think about all you have said, but I promise we will discuss things further."

"When, Papa? When may we talk again?" she asked eagerly.

He hesitated and walked towards the door.

"Give me two days. I think you will agree that I am an honest man, Charity."

"I know you are. Please believe me when I say that. But do try to see my point of view. I am sorry I was so rude and disobeyed your orders when I mentioned . . . when I . . ."

But the door had closed. She sank into her chair, shaken with fright at her boldness and obstinacy, but firm of purpose and prepared to do battle indomitably if necessary.

Matthew's behaviour next morning was as usual, with both his family and servants. None would believe, thought Charity, he had spent as she shrewdly believed a sleepless night beset with unexpected problems. Today was one of his Warwick days, necessitating the use of his carriage. Sometimes one of the girls would accompany him on that trip and visit the market town.

Today however, Charity was too busy with her restless thoughts and loth to seek her father's company until some agreement regarding her plans had been reached.

Mercy was engrossed in her own affairs. She had vanished to her room immediately after breakfast, a large thick envelope clutched in her hands, sparkling eyes belying her nonchalant manner. Both Charity and her father recognised the masculine handwriting. It was four months since Miles

THE HOUSE IN HOLLY WALK

had sailed away on that bright summer's day.

It was now November and a sharp rap on the rain-splashed kitchen door interrupted Charity's daily discussion with Cook. It was opened to admit a thin soaking youth, sodden cap in hand. Recognizing him as the garden help at the vicarage, Charity, removing his wet jacket, bade Polly bring a scalding mug of broth before enquiring his errand.

"Is there something wrong at the vicarage, Joshua?"

"Well I can't rightly say, Miss. Vicar seems all right and Mrs. Tafler an' all as fur as I can tell."

"The baby. Is the baby well?"

"Oh yes, Miss. Our Freda was doing for 'er when I left an' she were as lively as a cricket."

The thin young face grinned over the top of the steaming cup. 'Our Freda' was Joshua's elder sister and Faith's general maid.

"Well then?" she enquired.

The boy looked up. "Mrs. Tafler says can you come to the Vicarage right away. It's very 'portant."

Charity glanced at the streaming windows as the boy continued.

"Mrs. Tafler says to bring Miss Mercy an' all. She says not to waste time. Summat 'as to be settled before the Master gets 'ome."

Puzzled at the urgency Charity left the kitchen to find Mercy in her room. Together they dressed in long cloaks and their stoutest boots, and armed with the largest umbrella set out. Mercy asked a stream of questions to which there was no answer as they hurried through the wet streets.

Faith ushered them into the warmth of her home, removing their wet clothes. They could see the agitation on her face and although her advanced pregnancy was very apparent she hastily reassured them on that account.

When she spoke her voice shook.

"It's Hope. She's here."

An incredulous silence followed but before either girl could speak Faith went on.

"She arrived about an hour ago. Alfred had already gone on his calls but I knew I could rely on you to come."

"Of course. How is she . . . ?"

"Is she alone, or . . . ?"

"She is completely alone and apart from being rather thin is physically well. She doesn't seem unduly distressed but one can never tell with Hope, and she and I were not particularly close. Probably Mercy can get her to talk, I'll call her."

As their elder sister left the room two pairs of anxious eyes met, the one half fearful, the other seemingly calm. In less than a minute a familiar figure stood before them.

Mercy gave a tiny gasp and put her hand to her lips, but Charity trying not to show her concern moved forward impulsively.

"Hope, my dear, how lovely to see you."

With a slightly defiant rise of her head the sister stood in the shadow to disguise the eyes made red with weeping. Her fair hair was dull and unkempt, the round, formerly bright face pinched as she spoke through tremulous lips.

"Hello . . ." her voice broke. Then they were all clinging together, Mercy and Hope openly crying whilst tears glistened on the lashes of the more composed girls. At that moment they were completely united. Close, compassionate, sharing a happy reunion, lightening a burden of sorrow. Old slights and injuries were forgotten, there were no recriminations, no questions, no answers. Just the warm overwhelming happiness of being together again.

They seated Hope in a comfortable chair close to the small fire, studiedly ignoring her shabby gown with its tattered lace and the worn broken slippers. They waited for her to regain her composure, for the trembling hands to still and warmth to flow back into the ashen face. It took time for her to control her voice and when she started to speak none could believe the subdued slightly husky sound of humility was the gay laughter-filled voice of their once carefree sister.

She told her story quietly at first until emotion got the better of her and violent weeping filled the unbroken silence. Pityingly they strove to calm her and by degrees pieced together the incoherent tale.

She had taken the local coach to Birmingham and joined Harry immediately on leaving home. After a few glorious whirlwind days of shopping and preparations in London they had sailed together on an extensive tour of Switzerland, France and Italy. Whirling through several glamorous European capitals the ample legacy left by Harry's grandfather supplied adequate means for two. It had been so wonderful and they were so much in love. It was sunshine and flowers, romance and glory for a whole long enchanting year. And then they came back to England.

Leaving her in London, Harry had gone to Brighton to discuss future plans with his doting mother. It was on his return she sensed a change in their relationship. His mother, however enchanted by her handsome son, had been distinctly displeased by his behaviour abroad and made it perfectly clear there would be no more money forthcoming; his student days were over and he must somehow earn himself a living. The unexpected shock of this had changed Harry considerably. In very reduced circumstances they lived in Paddington for five weeks, constantly bickering, their undying love rapidly fading, and when eventually he left, she had no claim on him, for he had never married her.

The pathetic little tale came to a close with the face of the sorry victim buried in her hands. The other three sat silently appalled. It had never entered any of their heads that Hope was still unmarried. The shocking fact that she had lived out of wedlock with a man for over a year affected each girl separately.

Faith felt revulsion sweep over her and, although loth to admit it, her husband's prim scandalised face was uppermost in her mind.

THE HOUSE IN HOLLY WALK

Mercy's violet eyes were round with shocked indignation. She blamed Hope's lover with the clear uncomplicated attitude of her young nature and was immediately a staunch ally on her sister's behalf.

Only Charity was able to take the news calmly. Her dark eyes shrewdly hid her cynical thoughts and she was the first to recover, shaking the others sharply from their sympathetic indignation to more practical aid. She could see that Hope was in a highly nervous state, and felt no time should be lost in seeking a solution.

"We must think what next can be done," she stated briskly.

"Of course you must come back with us to Holly Walk," Mercy cried impulsively.

The stricken girl raised her head sharply, her voice shrill.

"I can't. Oh no, I couldn't face Papa, not yet. It is quite impossible." She turned to her elder sister. "Let me stay with you for a little while, please Faith."

Charity noticed how pale and miserably hesitant was her married sister's face.

"No," she said firmly. "It would not do. Faith has Alfred to consider and it is not fitting in the circumstances you should remain here." She looked thoughtful. "Papa will have to be told of course, but it must be thought out carefully. He is in Warwick today and is usually tired and touchy after the journey so will not be kindly disposed towards anything tonight."

Frantically Hope looked from one to the other and became almost hysterical.

"You must help me with Papa. I shall die if you leave me to face him alone."

Putting a steadying arm around the sobbing girl's shoulders, Faith rose.

"Don't worry, darling. You shall stay here for a few days even against Alfred's wishes if there is no other remedy."

"But there is another way," cried Mercy turning swiftly to Charity. "Why can't we smuggle her into Holly Walk? We can keep her there for at least two or three days and no one need ever know."

"I think you are right," nodded Charity. "Between us you and I can arrange that. We shall have to do it quietly after dark but somehow we will secrete her into the house until an arrangement can be made to enlighten Papa." She turned to the distressed girl. "You can stay in your old room. It is quite unused and infrequently cleaned. It should not be difficult to keep Polly away for a few days."

They sat discussing ways and means until Hope became calmer. Both she and Faith were uneasy, but the quiet assurance of Charity's and Mercy's boundless enthusiasm raised their flagging spirits enough to listen attentively to the plan. It was decided that a swift course of action would be best, and that very night when the house was still and an hour after Papa's usual bedtime, Mercy was to creep out and meet her sister half way. They would then proceed to Holly Walk together. It was unlikely that anyone in their district would be about at that hour, and Charity with a candle in her bedroom window would signal any necessary warning. Faith promised to keep Hope hidden from Alfred for a few hours in one of the empty rooms in the vicarage, but she was concerned for the girls being alone in the dark streets at such unwelcome hours. Hope, only too glad of a solution, accepted the plan gladly.

And so it was decided. But fate in the form of the elements was to take a hand and their carefully laid plans went awry.

Storms lashed the little town with increasing violence all afternoon and at half past four when Matthew returned from Warwick the wind had whipped to gale force with incessant driving rain.

With dusk the river burst its banks. Walled gardens in lower Holly Walk were submerged in a torrent of angry floods and all was hidden in the swirl of rushing water.

Matthew, rapidly recruiting Archer and the gardener's boy, battled towards a row of low-lying cottages. Nestling on the riverside at the far end of the Walk, they were dangerously near submersion.

"They'll be up to their necks in no time, sir," boomed Archer above the shrieking gale. "I only hope they have the sense to get out. There are women and at least half a dozen children down there to my knowledge."

Matthew nodded grimly. After struggling into

his ulster he had spoken rapidly to the girls.

"Heat up plenty of broth and prepare the kitchen for a number of people. Keep a good fire going."

Organising the kitchen staff and collecting odd clothing and blankets gave the girls plenty to do and little time for discussion, but as the evening wore on Mercy sought out Charity and asked anxiously about their plans.

"I can't think at the moment," came the whispered reply. "Perhaps the wind will drop. After all it is only eight o'clock. We have plenty of time yet."

But the gale did not cease, and neither did the river subside. The kitchen was full of shivering women and frightened children, their sodden clothes steaming by the big open range. Polly and Amy were distributing mugs of hot soup whilst Cook, red-faced and affronted, muttered at her disorganised domain. She baked appetising little rock buns however to thrust into thin eager hands.

The men, a sizeable force now from the town, were still working by the swollen river, rescuing cattle, shepherding floundering country folk, striving to dam the most vulnerable parts of the shallow disappearing banks.

In her quiet unruffled way, Charity soothed the scared anxious community. Many of them had known her gentle administrations on previous occasions as one crisis after another arose in their poverty-stricken households.

Mercy, following the older girl's example, was

warmed inwardly when rewarded by wan and grateful thanks from the refugees. It wasn't until fairly late in the evening she discovered Gyp was missing and became panic stricken. With the greatest difficulty Charity prevented her from rushing headlong out into the violent night in search of her pet. She ran backwards and forwards to the heavy oak door calling distractedly in her agitation. Charity, exhausted, and almost dropping with fatigue, gave a sigh of relief at Matthew's second appearance in the kitchen.

He was wet through, hands bleeding, nails broken, hair and face dripping with moisture. But he calmed his youngest daughter, promising a search party for the dog as soon as the men could be spared. He spoke kindly comforting words to the strange assortment of humanity gathered around his hearth and was unprepared for the blast of air as the kitchen door suddenly crashed open.

All eyes turned to a figure in the doorway. White-faced with unutterable weariness, clutching the struggling terrified Gyp in her arms, she seemed like a ghost from the past.

Bowed by the rain, the cruel wind raking her hair about her shoulders she met Matthew's gaze across the room levelly, dumbly appealing.

It was Hope.

SEVEN

A PALE CONTRITE sun the following morning filtered through grey clouds. Gone was the tempest of the previous night, but the havoc of the subsiding waters was devastating. An oozing stream of thick brown mud seemed to penetrate everywhere and very few establishments in the lower town had escaped damage.

The townfolk however faced it with the typical stoicism of the Midlander. In no time at all they set about draining off their land, re-housing their folk and finding temporary pastures for their beasts.

By noon the Glovers' kitchen was free of its overnight refugees. Alfred had organised temporary accommodation in the Church Hall for many ladies of the town donated blankets and parcels of clothing. Food was also sent from many a well stocked larder, but the smell of wet clothing and stale unwashed bodies hung around the Glovers' kitchen until Cook indignantly instructed Polly to prop open the heavy door and let in God's sweet, if undeniably damp air.

Upstairs Charity lay sleeping from sheer exhaustion fully clothed on her bed. It was an uneasy sleep for all her fatigue, and she woke shortly after noon, troubled and harassed as the night's events came flooding back to her. She could still see Hope standing in the doorway and the silence broken only by a glad cry from Mercy as she flew across the kitchen to snatch the frantic dog from her sister's arms. She could still see the stricken look on her father's face as she herself drew the exhausted figure into the sheltering warmth of the house. She had wrapped a shawl about the dripping shoulders and hastened the girl upstairs away from astonished eyes.

When she came down later, Mercy volunteered the information she sought: Papa, without comment, had gone straight out again into the night.

No more stragglers arrived and at dawn with everyone bedded down warm and safe she and Mercy looked in at their unhappy sister who lay sleeping quietly now, and at peace. Charity had then fallen on to her own bed, too tired to undress, but listening for her father's return. Only after hearing his voice murmuring to Archer as he mounted the stairs had she fallen asleep.

Now she glanced at the watch pinned to her bodice; it was after one o'clock, the morning gone! Hurriedly she washed and changed her creased gown before peeping into the room where Mercy still lay sleeping, her arm protectively over the warm contented body of Gyp. Neither stirred as she quietly closed the door.

The gently breathing figure of Hope had scarcely moved since last night. Still pretty, the long lashes casting shadows on her pale cheeks, she seemed indeed little changed. Charity stood looking at the fair unkempt hair; it would take some time to recover its former glory.

No sound penetrated through the solid oak of her father's door so, sighing slightly, she continued downstairs, refusing to dwell on any problems until the tasks for the day had been fulfilled.

Appearing from the pantry as she crossed the hall, Archer, in spite of a broken night and only limited sleep, was correct, faultlessly dressed, impeccable. Seeing her enquiring face he spoke.

"The Master was up at his usual time, Miss, and has gone to join the town's gentlemen. They were meeting at noon to discuss the situation."

"I see. Has anything been done for the flood victims?"

Archer assured her that the shepherding of the families to the Church Hall had already taken place. The relief she felt that at least one decision had been made overcame her, and as she entered the warm kitchen she sat down quickly at the freshly scrubbed table. She was horrified to feel tears of weakness pricking behind her eyelids and she shut them tightly from curious eyes. Cook sent Polly scuttling away and put a comforting hand on her shoulder. She spoke briskly with the familiarity of long service, clucking like an old hen over the girl, forcing her to drink a cup of hot strong tea, and buttered some scones so that they dripped appetisingly under her nose.

THE HOUSE IN HOLLY WALK

She sat alone with Cook who worked silently at her pastry, understanding the girl's need for solitude. The familiar smell of baking and the crackle of the fire presented harmony where but a few hours before chaos had reigned. Fresh strength gradually flowed through her and again she was prepared to face the oncoming difficulties of the very near future.

Her own plans were thrust aside with resolve and any further discussions with her father must be postponed until the more urgent question of Hope was settled. How he would react to the sudden reappearance of his wayward daughter she could not imagine.

Her troubled thoughts were broken by the sound of his voice as he unexpectedly appeared below stairs.

"I will have a cold dinner sent up if you please, Cook," he requested, before turning to his daughter.

"Perhaps you will be good enough to join me, my dear. You need food to sustain you after the catastrophic night."

He took her arm, concerned at her fatigue, and solicitous of her comfort refused to enter into any serious conversation until they had eaten, he satisfied, and she composed.

He studied her thoughtfully, and when he spoke his voice though stern was not unkind as he demanded her own knowledge of Hope's return during last night's storm.

Charity answered him, relating the meeting of yesterday afternoon and their conspiracy.

"I didn't dream she would be silly enough to leave the vicarage in such weather, but she told me later she was determined to carry out our plan. She was so afraid Alfred would discover her presence, particularly as they were preparing all the spare rooms for the flood victims. She knew how shocked he would be if he found that Faith had deceived him. You must allow she behaved well over that, Papa. She felt she had caused us all enough grief, and even at the risk of drowning she meant to do her utmost to get here."

"Stupid girl. What good would have come by throwing her life away?"

"I feel she behaved bravely, Papa, whatever you may say, and she did rescue Gyp when he was being swept under the bridge."

Her father agreed. "I will grant her that. Now I want to know in her exact words, as you remember them, the story of her life since leaving this house in August last year."

Charity told him then, omitting nothing of her sister's story. The joys, the sorrows, the final disillusion were all poured forth, only to be interrupted now and again by a muttered sharp word from Matthew . . . "blackguard . . . defiler . . . my lost child."

He had turned from her, looking out of the window on to the desolate garden. He sat so long she wondered if he had forgotten her presence. But Charity had the gift of stillness, so she sat waiting, her breathing soft and unnoticed in the silence.

Suddenly he swivelled his chair to face her and began to speak slowly and with emphasis.

"You must realise that during the past months things have not been easy for me. I have, I hope, hidden from you all the extent of my feelings towards Hope and the shame and unhappiness she has brought upon us all. I am aware that many of our friends have speculated on the disappearance of one of our united family, as you being a member must fully appreciate.

"However, lately I have, I must admit, felt grave misgivings and anxieties concerning the fate of your sister and have longed to withdraw my disciplinary action. I have felt very much the need to have her with us again, and frequently the urge to discuss the matter with you has occurred to me. Why I refrained I cannot say. Call it pride and the inability to accept my mistake if you will. When I saw her standing in the doorway last night I thought my heart would break, she looked so ill and desolate, so vulnerable. And yet a great elation swept through me so that I could do nothing but hurry away until my feelings were under control."

"Oh, Papa. I am so glad."

He smiled faintly at her, but a sterner note crept into his voice.

"You will understand now I am willing to take her back into the fold, but on no account is there to be a fatted calf. It will take me time to forgive her completely and I think stern discipline must be exercised for some time. You will say she has suffered enough and quite rightly too, but we all learn by experience, and I shall expect cooperation and not a little submission from that young lady.

"I will explain a scheme I have in mind. I want

you to train Hope to take over your tasks. Teach her all you know, how to run the house well and efficiently, and, if given time she succeeds, I shall feel our efforts and encouragement have been worth while."

Hardly daring to breathe, with her hopes trembling on the brink, Charity faltered.

"You want her to take over the house?"

"Why not? Now is the time to prove her worth. I have given some thought to the plans you proposed to me a few days ago, and providing Hope is a willing pupil, and providing your health is sound enough, I see no reason why you should not go to London for a short time as you wish. It is now seven weeks to Christmas and, with the necessary preparations already under way, Hope will benefit and I believe show some competence. If all goes well in the New Year, proposals for your new venture may go ahead."

"Thank you, Papa."

She gazed up at him, a slow flush of pleasure lighting up her pale face. She put out one of her hands impulsively and slipped it into his resting on the table.

"I don't know what to say. I am so grateful."

He patted the little hand gently, perhaps for the first time feeling an affinity with her.

"I have pride in your qualities, my dear, and appreciate your values. I hope the future brings all you desire. Now I shall have a long talk with Hope and am confident that before long a closer bond will exist between us."

EIGHT

The shroud of sorrow had vanished from the house, and it blossomed as though reborn. Preparations for the annual festivities were in full swing.

After a long and serious morning closeted with her father, Hope emerged subdued and chastened, but with her old sparkle very near the surface. The interview was a closed book, a secret matter between the two of them.

Matthew allowed her a few new strictly serviceable gowns. He warned her to expect no further additions apart from a thick cloak and very austere bonnets for marketing.

The other girls delved into their trunks and produced ribbons and fichus of dainty Brussels lace to trim the bonnets when visiting friends. That the culprit carried off these occasions with discretion and would sit meekly silent beneath curious glances was a source of amazement to Mercy. She suspected the downcast lashes hid a glint of amusement and perhaps an impish delight at the furore she caused in otherwise dignified drawing-rooms.

Mercy remembered with delight Aunt Lydia's last Christmas parcel, and the exotic Indian shawl it contained, together with the prettiest velvet slippers were most welcome. Hope's golden hair was washed, brushed and polished by Mercy with a piece of silk until it soon regained its former glory. Within a few weeks the sparse figure filled out, and once more the eye-catching beauty of former days unfolded like a gay butterfly.

The household duties so painstakingly explained by Charity were tackled contritely and with a humbleness irrelevant to Hope's nature. But in spite of frequent bursts of frustration she persevered and managed gradually to achieve some success. She was dejected by her father's attitude; his stern watchful eyes dismayed her and she wondered how long it would take to regain his trust.

Charity showed endless patience and was anxious not to appear over-eager, for although none but Matthew shared her secret plans, honesty forbade her overlooking the smallest detail.

Mercy was like a ray of light, eager to help Hope and to learn the rudiments of management herself. She could not believe things were back to normal, that life was again beautiful and the past dreary nightmare months over.

To allow Charity more time with Hope, she herself took over much of the welfare work, and would set off on her bounteous errands with Gyp bounding gleefully at her heels, the early morning frosty air giving both girl and dog sparkling energy.

Matthew himself was content. He knew only too soon his heart would melt before the unfamiliar timidity of Hope's approach to him, and soon she would again be pulling his beard with precocious teasing as only she dare do. He put resolutely from his mind that a change in her physically was a damage beyond repair. She was no longer a virgin and unsullied by the world, but he felt when the time came for a suitable husband to be found for her the bitter experience she had suffered should bring to any marriage a better understanding.

Archer had settled matters below stairs. The servants might well talk among themselves, but Matthew's private domain would be protected from gossip. Friends might have proved difficult but his usual inscrutability and aloofness caused speculation to gradually subside. It sufficed that Hope was back and it ill became sharp eyes to question, or curiosity to cause a tongue to wag too long. He had confidence in his girls too; they were intensely loyal and would stand staunchly together whatever situation arose.

Frequently since their talk in November his thoughts had dwelt on Charity, and as she moved about the house keeping her own counsel he watched her with increasing wonder. He should never have underestimated this one. Behind that quiet mouselike exterior was a staunch heart carrying a banner for the underdog, working purposefully and inconceivably towards her goal.

On Christmas morning the first large snowflakes began to fall, but the congregation at All Souls were tightly packed and warmly wrapped against the east wind. Everywhere was an air of festivity. The pulpit was decorated with red-berried holly, and Christmas roses sent from Matthew's greenhouse gleamed like jewels among the glossy leaves. The Glover pew was filled with family and servants all proudly beaming, for this morning at precisely five o'clock, the very day of our Saviour's birth, Faith was safely delivered of her second child, another girl, but welcome, and received thankfully into a loving home. Alfred, almost dropping with fatigue, preached a glowing sermon of thanks for which he was praised highly amid congratulations following the service.

The rest of the day was happy and peaceful. Matthew, filled with a sense of well-being, accompanied his daughters to the vicarage to see the wan but triumphant Faith. Then an early night was welcomed by all for on the following day a grand party was to be held with their friends and relations fathering *en masse* under the roof at Holly Walk.

Charity had worked long and hard to make this event a success, and, although Hope did her best to assist her, tapping feet and sparkling eyes were already anticipating the dancing Papa had permitted them to arrange. The Pump Room string orchestra had been engaged and a promise of the new waltzes by Mr. Strauss was greatly anticipated. Mercy felt they were really living fast and furiously, as the Queen had only recently allowed the waltzes at Court, and such an early introduction into their own small unknown town was fame indeed.

Papa presented them each with a new gown, and relenting his earlier harshness had included Hope in this gesture. As they paraded before him however he noticed how much more extravagant was her blue crinoline than those worn by the other girls. Nevertheless, he was pleased at their delightful appearance and resplendent himself in a new velvet jacket led the mazurka with his eldest present daughter, his coat tails and thick hair flying.

It was a happy time and one Charity was to remember in the months to come, when her life changed beyond recognition.

On the second day of the New Year, Papa called her into the library and gravely and thoroughly discussed her plans. She found it much easier now to lay them before him, and it was decided she would leave on the fifteenth of the month for London. He had favoured above the other charities Miss Nightingale's programme and felt that nursing would be less strenuous and distressing than other unpleasant and often dangerous administrations in the slums.

On the date set Matthew arranged to accompany her in his own carriage to London, and preparations were immediately set afoot. Charity herself asked for everything to be as simple as possible. All her needs were packed into a single trunk and even that was half filled with books. She insisted on taking only bare essentials, warm clothing and stout boots, cotton dresses and aprons for warmer days, but no unnecessary encumbrances. She refused to consider her new lilac dress and bequeathed it to Hope, but Mercy snatched it angrily away, declaring fiercely Charity would need it again herself when she returned home in the not too distant future.

Hope flounced off as Polly put her head around the door with a message from Cook. Mercy sat quietly alone gazing into the fire, her sewing lying idly in her lap. She felt suddenly an intense loneliness sweep over her; Charity's serene calm presence would be unbearably missed. Often one was unaware of her as she moved about the house until unexpectedly the grave presence would be there to shoulder one's problems and solve the trials of the day. It was only during the months of Hope's absence that she herself began to appreciate Charity, to respect the resolute loyalties and strength of her character. With Charity's going it seemed a chapter would be closed.

What was in store for herself? She was eighteen years old and chafed at the thought that most of her life had been spent in Holly Walk. She was happy and loved her home, Gyp, and walking in the luscious green countryside, but since last summer how often her thoughts turned secretly to a young officer in Her Majesty's Bengal Army. How often she had taken out the little book Miles had given her, searching among the marked poems for a sign of love and hope.

They corresponded regularly. His letters were long and chatty, full of interesting facts about that far distant fascinating country, and she replied in much the same way, telling him all the humdrum gossip of the little town. But there was nothing even suggesting romance, and she began to wonder if those few halcyon days were a fantasy and the whispered words on his departure only a dream. He begged for a picture of her and Papa allowed her to send a miniature of herself painted a few years ago, in which she privately thought she looked absurdly young. He sent in return a portrait of himself executed by a native artist, looking extraordinarily handsome in his scarlet jacket with plumed hat tucked beneath his arm.

Hope was most impressed and remarked on his distinguished appearance.

"I just can't wait to meet him," she enthused, glancing at her own reflection in the mirror speculatively.

When this happy day would come Mercy had no idea. Papa felt in regard to diplomatic relations abroad it would possibly be several years.

Matthew was in London three days, arriving back exhausted and slightly irritable. Yes, Charity was well, he replied in answer to their eager questions; she seemed to settle with remarkable ease in an odd little house in Bloomsbury. Yes, he had seen the women's hospital where she was to commence her training: it was gaunt and ugly and cold. Yes, he had met Miss Nightingale and she seemed a very formidable young woman; he had no doubt any female under her protective wing would be in safe keeping.

Frequent letters from Charity came in the early part of the year. Some were long, revealing epistles of life in the poorest parts of London and of nursing and study under Miss Nightingale's tuition. Always there were words of praise and admiration for that determined and extraordinary woman born out of her time. From her training in Germany and Paris she had established such revolutionary ideas in the London hospitals as to evoke disapproval and anger among many prominent dignitaries and statesmen of the day.

Sometimes Charity's letters were short and obviously hurriedly written between long arduous hours on duty. Then fatigue quite often showed in the hastily written lines, but her promise to keep in touch each week was faithfully kept, and as time went on the pattern of routine was accepted by Matthew and the girls without question.

War in the Crimea was declared in February, which Matthew predicted gloomily, was a disaster and one likely to cause considerable misery and hardship in England and the allied countries in spite of being a comfortable distance away on Russian soil.

With June an unexpected pleasure came Mercy's way. Matthew had quite unexpectedly decided to make a two-day visit to London and declared his intention of taking her along. He naturally had appointments in the city, but he also wished to call on Charity and find out for himself how she was faring in her dubious occupation. He planned to leave Mercy with her for a few hours whilst his business affairs were conducted, and he felt that by doing so he would learn more of Charity's new way of life. The two girls would undoubtedly chatter at great length and Mercy could be relied upon to put his uneasy mind at rest regarding her sister's health.

Mercy was delighted at the thought of seeing Charity again. She flew about the house preparing her best clothes and packing a small valise with her immediate needs.

Hope was outwardly envious and not a little put out to think that she was being left behind. However the look in her father's eye forbade any display of temper and she made the best of it by deciding that certain articles in her wardrobe needed replenishing. Snippets of ribbons, buttons and bindings were carefully labelled for Mercy to match in the great London shops.

NINE

MERCY AND HER father stayed in a comfortable hotel in the Strand, far enough from the noise and smoke to be pleasant, but near enough to the interesting crowded streets to delight Mercy. She was allowed a certain amount of freedom during the hours Papa was closeted in a stuffy office in Throckmorton Street. She was pleased that Matthew was enlightened enough to grant her a few hours alone in the grand emporiums with which London was graced, convinced that she would come to no harm.

The evening they arrived they called at the house in Bloomsbury, only to find Charity was on hospital duty in Paddington. Matthew, not to be outdone, proceeded there and when refused admission fought a frigid but triumphant battle with a poker-faced matriarch who allowed them only five minutes with the flushed agitated girl. It seemed preposterous to Matthew that his own daughter was inaccessible when they had travelled so far to visit her.

THE HOUSE IN HOLLY WALK

He grumbled persistently during the drive back to their hotel.

"Such discipline is worse than the army," he growled. "I am much inclined to take her home again."

"Don't suggest that, Papa," begged Mercy, knowing how her sister would react. "She is really dedicated to her work and I am sure she could never give it up now. She was promised a whole day off on Thursday so we have that to look forward to. I can entertain myself tomorrow as you will be so busy."

Matthew frowned.

"It is unfortunate I have so many commitments. I am beginning to wonder if I did the right thing in bringing you at all," he mused. "Very well, my dear, don't distress yourself. It is simply that I feel it will be a long day for you and time may lie heavy on your hands."

"Nonsense, Papa. I shall enjoy every minute of it. I have several purchases to make in the morning; I really don't know how I shall manage to find all the trifles Hope asked me to get. In the afternoon a walk by the river will be lovely."

"You must promise not to wander too far alone," Matthew interrupted sharply. "London customs are different from provincial ways you know, and it may not be wise for you to walk the streets alone."

"I will be very careful. If Charity can safely visit the heart of the East End, then surely no harm will befall me in a busy thoroughfare on a summer's afternoon."

"There is a quality about Charity that makes her accepted wherever she goes, and remember her calling can open many a door denied to others. You must regard my wishes on this matter and take care."

Mercy assented and the next afternoon found her, shopping done, sitting on the Embankment watching the stream of barges and sailing craft busily moving up and down the Thames. There was so much to see and do in this entrancing place called London. Hyde Park, Rotten Row, and the Royal Palaces had yet to be seen, but it was restful to sit idly and think in the midst of the bustling throng of Miles and the letter she had received a few days before.

For the first time since his departure last year he spoke of coming home. For the first time had written "Dearest Mercy" instead of "Dear Friend." Her heart fluttered as she recalled his closing sentence, "Love, Miles."

She hugged the secret words to her in joyous anticipation. How often had she impatiently scanned his letters for a sign; how often had she longingly thought of last summer and the dream they had started. Had she read more into their relationship than was intended? He had never yet told her he loved her, but surely the warmth of his words lately meant more than friendship and she clung to the slender thread of hope fiercely. His writing had entertained them all with its humour and spontaneity, but only the most recent pages were for her alone. When he returned to England she would know soon enough if the yearning she felt with every fibre of her body was to be fulfilled.

She was too engrossed with her thoughts to notice a nearby figure contemplating her until a voice spoke her name.

"I just cannot believe it. It *is* Miss Mercy, isn't it? Or should I say Miss Glover now you are really grown up? Let me see, it must be quite two years since last we met."

Flustered, she gazed up at the man before her, so close, so overwhelming—a ghost from the past.

"Harry," she gasped, "Harry Bettridge."

Her first thought was to fly from the cynical face before her but as she made to rise he put out a restraining arm.

"Please don't get up. It's such a pleasure to see you. May I sit here?"

As he waited, Mercy from the other end of the bench gave a small nod of assent while she desperately strove to control her agitation under his quizzical look, and a swift indignation at his presence was rapidly overtaking her. She sat very still.

"How well you look, Mercy. I hope I'll be forgiven for saying you are becoming a very attractive young lady. It wouldn't surprise me to see you develop into the greatest beauty of them all one day."

Try as she might she could not prevent her colour rising as his cool eyes laughed at her confusion.

"Are your sisters well?" he asked. "And your father, still the honourable citizen of your splendid town? I expect he has risen to the heights of Mayor by now. What of my dear cousin Alfred and his bride?" He laughed. "Naturally, bride no longer as I believe they now have a child."

Mercy could scarcely believe this was happening and anger swept over her as she regarded his long legs stretched comfortably and the gay eyes glinting at her. Harry Betteridge, the dissolute rake, the ruination of Hope, the cause of unspeakable anguish to all her loved ones—how dare he approach her like a long lost friend? He was speaking again.

"I asked about my cousin and his family. Have they a boy or a girl?"

"Two," she answered shortly, "both girls."

She got to her feet collecting her parcels rapidly, but he was before her and broke in.

"You are not leaving me—so soon."

"I have nothing further to say to you. Please excuse me; Papa. . . ."

"So he is in London too. Are you visiting the glamorous Lady Asterling again?"

"My aunt is in India now. We are staying in a hotel."

"Then do allow me to walk with you. Is it far?"

She turned away from him.

"Not far. I prefer to go alone. Kindly leave me; my father would be very angry if he saw you."

Ignoring her request he began to walk beside her, and short of running in an unseemly fashion she could do nothing but accept his company.

"Don't be alarmed. I shall naturally keep well out of your father's way. Much has happened since I saw him last on Alfred's wedding day. I am glad things are well with them."

She peeped quickly at him, trying to detect a sneer in his voice, and expected to receive a mocking glance, but he was looking ahead and his face was inscrutable.

"I have a son of my own, you see."

Surprised, her eyes flew open to be hastily averted as his own turned to her.

"You are surprised? Hasn't Hope mentioned him, or isn't she back at home with you after all?"

"Oh yes, she's back; she came home last November. But why should she mention your son?"

"Considering he is her son too, I find that quite astounding," he murmured.

Mercy stopped dead among the hurrying throng and Harry drew her against the parapet and turned her face towards the river. Her hands shook as she nervously plucked at her bonnet strings.

"I don't know what you mean."

The laugh he gave was short and mirthless.

"Surely it is perfectly obvious, Mercy. Jonathan, my son, is ten months old; I am his father and your dear sister Hope is his mother."

During the sudden stillness he waited for her agitation to pass. She forced herself to look at him. The mocking eyes were steady and there was a foreign soberness about his mouth.

"Yes, Hope is his mother."

She had to strain to catch the softly spoken words.

"He is so like her—fair, enchanting, with the

bluest eyes imaginable."

Bewildered she stood, mesmerised by the slow moving waters beneath them. Tears of shock and sorrow pricked behind her eyes.

"I can't believe it—and yet I suppose I must. You were together then. . . ."

"In Switzerland. He was born there. We had hoped to return to England before the birth but it was a few weeks premature so we had to stay."

"Hope! She is so helpless and spoilt and afraid of sickness. How did she endure childbirth?"

"Oh, she endured! Believe me, my dear, your sister is as strong as a horse and twice as frisky. She sailed through the birth with very little effort and was back on her feet and ready for dancing in less than two weeks."

"But where is the baby now?" Agonizingly she looked at him. "You left her. She told us you left her. Did you take the baby away too?"

"You have heard Hope's version of the story and a very good one it is I'm sure. But surely you know your sister well enough to understand how easily she deceives and how boldly those blue eyes hide the most bare-faced lies when it suits her. I may be a rogue and a womaniser, but I loved her; I loved her intensely. She is the mother of my son and I am never likely to forget that. Like all doting fathers, to me he is the cleverest, most wonderful, child in the world."

"But what about marriage? Why didn't you marry her?"

"Do you think I didn't try?" he answered savagely. "As soon as I knew she was pregnant I begged on my knees." He grimaced oddly. "I, on my knees, Harry Betteridge the philanderer! But I felt in spite of our many adversities we could with our child make a success of life together. She refused me, of course. My financial position was very insecure and I came to know that money was extremely important to Hope. It may be difficult to believe, and who am I to expect your trust and understanding, but is it likely I would desert them both? Make no mistake, Mercy, I know where my responsibilities lie."

She knew the truth; oh how she knew it. Hope, selfish, shallow, her mind filled with fripperies would not want the encumbrance of a child.

"She left you." Her voice was only a whisper. "She left you both, you and the baby. He must have been very tiny then."

"Three months." He shrugged. "I have no wish to hear the story she fabricated, but when she found we could no longer live on love alone it was the end for her."

"How could she do it? How could she leave her baby?" She looked wistfully over the river. "Papa would have adored a grandson, especially Hope's child. Oh Harry, I am so sorry."

He turned to her and expertly retied her tangled bonnet strings.

"Don't worry, my dear. Jonathan and I are managing very well. It is surprising how many doting ladies are around when they see an eligible bachelor trying to raise a very small child alone. They haven't all been ladies either. More often than not the kindest hearts are found among the lowest creatures. However things are different now; I have an excellent housekeeper who is devoted to the boy. I am away most of the day myself actually earning a living! It is a very respectable, tedious job but it makes me, to my sorrow, a dull but honest man."

A flicker of the old whimsical charm flashed out and she knew even in his most serious moments it would never be far away.

"I would love to see the baby," she said with longing.

"Perhaps, one day. We shall see. Now, don't you think we had better hurry along? You must not cause your father any anxiety."

"Oh, goodness. I wonder what time it is, have you a watch?"

Harry reassured her of the time and to ease her worried mind he questioned her as they walked along about family and their mutual friends. She found herself telling him of Charity's venture, about Papa's interest in the railways, and how well Hope was surviving the domesticities of Holly Walk.

"She seems to quite enjoy it now she has resigned herself to a quiet life and hardly put out at all when Papa suggested I should come on the London trip, leaving her behind."

She failed to see the sceptical look in Harry's eyes as she spoke loyally of her sister, quite without any obvious motives but hoping perhaps to soften some of the bitterness in the man's heart.

He let her talk, murmuring now and then in reply, but guiding her along where necessary with a firm hand, realising her sense of unease and shock. She did not cringe from the touch of his lips on her gloved hands as he raised it in farewell.

Fortunately Papa was not yet back, and she entered their quiet rooms thankfully, removing her outdoor things and freshening her face in the clear cool water by her bedside. How was she to control the turmoil of her thoughts? How to face Papa with a calm unguarded face, answering the trivial questions he would inevitably ask about her day? Happily they had tickets for the opera this evening so the long hours would be filled without too much conversing and the darkness of the Opera House would, she hoped, conceal her troubled eyes.

Covent Garden and the thought of her first visit to this famous house of music and entertainment had so thrilled and excited her, and she was determined nothing should spoil it. Then tomorrow must be Charity's day. She knew instinctively that there would be very few hours in the future to be frittered away together. Her sister's work was creating an irretrievable separation between them. Her heart was wrapped up in her worthy cause and the hours spent with her family would be precious indeed.

She refused to think of Hope and her extraordinary behaviour until she returned to Holly Walk. How could she be faced and what would ensue remained to be seen. Sufficient that the immediate days ahead were here to be enjoyed.

The opera was a joy to behold as the scenes

changed dramatically and the heavenly voices soared aloft, while the audience, glittering with diamonds was breathtaking.

The dreaded sleepless hours did not materialise, for when they returned it was late, and flushed with two glasses of unaccustomed Madeira wine Papa insisted on her taking in honour of the occasion, she simply fell into bed and thankfully into a deep dreamless sleep.

Matthew had ordered a carriage to collect Charity at ten o'clock next morning and she was with them very soon. How wonderful it was to see her; her animation was completely natural and the long arduous hours of duty failed to dull the warmth and pleasure in her eyes. She entertained them as she talked happily of the brighter side of her work and the Spartan living conditions they had to endure were dismissed lightly. Privately Mercy, who yesterday had glimpsed the Nurses' accommodation, considered the rooms little more than cells where only the barest essentials were allowed, and the contents extremely scanty and austere.

Matthew thought she looked thinner than ever and questioned her eating habits. She assured him the food supplied was good and wholesome and said how often she felt ashamed to eat at all considering the appalling hunger rife in many parts of the city.

Matthew refused to be drawn to the East End, so the afternoon was spent admiring the parks and the splendour of magnificent buildings. While driving back to the hospital Charity told them of her plans to take up permanent residence there.

THE HOUSE IN HOLLY WALK

She found traveling to and from Bloomsbury each day tedious and was often too tired to even bother with the journey, but would snatch a few hours' sleep on the day beds supplied for this purpose. She told them how valiantly Miss Nightingale was fighting for permission to install her women in men's hospitals and even to get nurses to the war front. She gave them facts and figures of the Crimean war that Matthew found astounding. He was disturbed that a well brought up young woman like his daughter should even know the numbers of soldiers embarking, let alone the amount of dead and mutilated bodies already filtering back to England.

He looked askance at the enthusiastic face, the quiet capable hands, as she spoke earnestly but without complaint of the terrible work stretching before herself and her staunch companions. He knew without doubt they had lost her. She had found her vocation, and sickness, disease and compassion had claimed her whole life. With pride and sorrow he became resigned to the fact she would never again live contentedly under his roof at Holly Walk.

TEN

FORTUNATELY FEW people were travelling when they left London for home and Matthew, after a few desultory remarks to his daughter, retired behind his copy of the *Railway Times*, thinking with satisfaction how successful his business deals had proved. In spite of ominous news of the far distant Crimea, rail shares were rising steadily, and he stood to gain substantially by them as long as a steel shortage did not prevent the extension of tracks. He pondered irritably on the considerable amount of iron needed for arms in this unnecessary and tragic war.

Had he known of Mercy's thoughts he would not have been quite so complacent. She was earnestly thinking of the problems before her. She could no longer thrust her new-found knowledge from her mind. What depths were there in the sister she thought she knew so well? Growing up in the other's company she had often been aware of her shortcomings, but never had it occurred to her that beneath the shallowness was such a deceptive heart.

Naturally she had kept the previous afternoon's disclosures from Papa. She had been sorely tempted to confide in Charity but the opportunity never arose. She had to see Hope before anything further could be done. Although hers was not a vindictive nature, she felt justifiable triumph at the thought of confronting her sister with her secret knowledge. Watching the startled eyes would give her immense satisfaction. She expected denials and hysterics, but trembled to think how violently Hope would undoubtedly react. There were hidden depths in the nature she had once thought light and superficial. Such knowledge would cause her to be over suspicious in future of the other's every move. Gone now was the trust, love and companionship of twenty years.

And as for Harry himself? Could a man, loving a child as devotedly as he loved his son, be wholly bad? It did not occur to her to question his story. In spite of his notorious past she believed him implicitly. There had been a sincerity in his behaviour that inspired her complete confidence.

Archer was waiting with the carriage and as they drew up at the front door Hope flew down the steps to greet them. Before they could remove their outdoor things she fired them with questions and seemed genuinely pleased to have them home.

Matthew answered her queries patiently, presenting her with a silver reticule she had desired. At supper, Mercy, trying to appear natural, secretly watched her sister, noting the glittering eyes and prattling tongue critically. Did she imagine an agitation in the quick-silver movements, and was there a suppressed hysteria close to the surface? How knowledge sharpens the wits of scrutiny. She was seeing things now that in her ignorance had previously been denied.

She slipped away to her room early, knowing that Hope and her father would be content with each other's company. The unpleasant interview was, she felt guiltily, being shelved.

The next day brought events that were to startle the little town and shatter whatever peace was left in Mercy's mind.

Both girls knew something unusual had occurred when Archer interrupted their father at breakfast. Matthew took his manservant into the library and did not reappear. Amy was so obviously quivering with excitement when clearing the table that Mercy enquired the cause.

"Well, Miss, we heard in the kitchen, when Mr. Palmer brought the milk, there's been a murder!"

"Murder. Where?"

"Down on the river path, near the bridge. Not a quarter of a mile from the garden gate 'ere."

"Good gracious. Have you any idea who it might be?"

Amy shook her head. "It's a man, but they don't know who it is yet. I do 'ear there was plenty of blood," she added with relish.

"That's enough, Amy." Hope stopped her sharply. "Get on with your work."

She beckoned Mercy into the hall, speaking calmly.

"It's no use getting into a state about this even

if there is some truth in the gossip. It was probably a tramp trespassing on someone's property. We shall have to wait until Papa comes home to hear the details. I want you to give Cook some instructions for me; I can't attend to them myself as I need to ride over to Radford. You don't mind do you? After all I have been more or less tied to the house for the last three days."

She sounded resentful and Mercy assured her she would carry out the domestic arrangements willingly. But she asked the reason for her visit to the outlying village of Radford Semele.

"Nancy Ingram has announced her engagement," replied Hope, "and I've promised to discuss the wedding plans with her."

"Nancy? How lovely. When is the wedding to be, and to whom?"

"It's Percy Adler, and there's no need to be facetious," Hope replied tartly as she saw Mercy's face twitch. The younger girl was remembering Faith's wedding day not so very long ago when she had teased Hope herself about that particular young man.

"I hope to be back by noon. If you go walking with Gyp I suggest you keep away from the river; it is sure to be swarming with local ghouls."

Mercy had an uneasy feeling that for some reason Hope was avoiding her, then shrugged it off as unlikely as she went to seek Cook.

At that moment Matthew entered the hall and seeing her he called:

"I see Jim is saddling the cob. Is it for Hope?"

"Yes, Papa, she is riding over to the Ingrams.

Nancy is getting married you know."

"So I believe. Will you please come into the library, Mercy. I have something to say to you."

Her father moodily paced the carpet as he spoke.

"I presume you have heard of the murder committed a short distance from our garden?"

She nodded and asked, "Have they discovered his identity yet?"

"They have indeed and, unpleasant as the business may be, the most astounding thing is that Harry Betteridge appears to be the unfortunate victim."

There was a stillness in the room that seemed to daze Mercy as she looked at her father in disbelief.

"What! What did you say?" she whispered.

There was no reason why Matthew should feel concern for her; he stood at the window and spoke half to himself.

"I suppose it is cowardly of me not to inform her myself, but I simply cannot discuss that creature dead or alive with Hope."

He turned to face her. "I feel, my dear, it may come more easily from you. As sisters you have always been close and I am sure you will find words to cause her as little distress as possible."

Mercy moistened her lips. "Are you sure it is Harry, Papa?"

"Of course I'm sure, child. He was found on the river bank and may have been there some days. Why he was in the vicinity is a mystery, but I certainly refuse to consider that Hope was involved. Alfred as next of kin had to establish his identity which naturally upset him—they are cousins remember. But he tells me the fellow did not call on them at the vicarage."

At his daughter's silence Matthew frowned and looked so closely at her serious face that she was forced to speak.

"You want me to break the news to Hope," she said.

"I realise it is an odious task but feel certain you are capable of explaining the situation without alarming her unnecessarily. Be as gentle as you can; she may need some comfort."

Comfort! Mercy had never known such bitterness as flowed involuntarily through her. Whenever had Hope given comfort to them, or anyone else she professed to love. How little had she cared for Harry and the child. Oh God, the baby ... what had become of the baby? Was he dead too?

Endless questions whirled inside her head and the confusion she felt stupefied her until she suddenly became aware of Matthew's sharp voice.

"Come along, Mercy, there is no need to be so upset on your sister's account. As I have already remarked, I trust her implicitly and am confident she would have no further dealings with such a character. Unfortunately my office duties now call —the morning has been too long wasted. Later I shall appreciate your remarks on Hope's reactions, but I feel all will be well and we can now treat the affair as a closed book."

Feeling slightly hysterical Mercy saw the irony of his concern for Hope and as she ran up to her room the tears overflowed. Her heart was heavy with grief for the dead man and fears for a little lost child. Papa had called it a closed book. But not for her, never for her until the whole miserable secret had been unravelled.

How could she forget the conversation she had held but days ago with the murdered man? She failed to understand why he had so suddenly come to the Midlands after their unexpected meeting. Was it solely to see once more the girl he had so adored, knowing her to be alone in the house at that particular time? Was it perhaps to discuss their child's future? Whatever the cause he must have had perfectly good reasons, but had the purpose of seeing Hope been achieved before his untimely death?

Hope, enlarging on the details of her friend's wedding, helped Mercy through the dinner they ate together and afterwards, telling Amy not to disturb them, she shut the dining-room door firmly against all intruders.

Sitting opposite the enquiring face of her sister, Mercy told her simply and clearly the facts she had learned from Matthew, without faltering. Feeling no compassion she watched relentlessly until Hope bowed her head and covered her eyes with her hands; those careless cruel little hands that could wring a man's heart without pity. Silently, stonily the younger girl surveyed the bent golden head before her, then suddenly she leaned forward and snatched the hands away. The blue eyes she met were cold and dry and any sympathy that might have arisen was frozen in Mercy's breast.

"Well, Hope?"

"What is there to say?" the other replied.

"What indeed." A feeling of despair overcame Mercy and she felt she must be ruthless to penetrate her sister's brain. "Don't you understand what I've said? Harry's been killed; they found him lying face down in a ditch. How could he have been so close to our home without your knowledge? Are you sure you did not see him?"

"Of course I didn't see him. Why should I? Our life together is over and as far as I am concerned he has been dead to me for months."

"Well I think you are completely heartless," Mercy burst out passionately, "speaking of someone you once loved in that horrible way. Don't you care at all?"

Rising, Hope smoothed her skirt. "I don't wish to discuss it further. You may of course tell Papa not to worry on my account. I am not defenceless, as I am quite sure he knows, and after all the sordid affair has nothing whatever to do with the family."

She moved towards the door and Mercy rose and shouted in a way she had never in her life done before.

"Sit down. I haven't finished yet."

Hope paused at the tone of her voice and controlling herself Mercy went on. "There is the small matter of your child."

Only the soft ticking of the clock broke the stillness, but Mercy watching intently saw the wide eyes fly open and a half-smothered gasp made her sister's voice shrill.

"What nonsense is this? Have you taken leave of your senses, or have the disgusting events of the past few hours affected your brain?"

"Neither." Mercy kept her voice firm while she told the other quietly of her meeting with Harry and what had ensued.

"You can understand the fright and horror I felt to learn of his death after seeing him so recently, and I am worried about the baby."

"Oh for Heaven's sake, Mercy. I cannot believe even you would be so gullible as to be taken in by such a feeble story."

There was not a waver of doubt in Mercy's mind as she answered. "I have never regarded Harry Betteridge as being particularly sincere, indeed I never knew him well enough. But I do believe he told me the truth in this matter. What reason would he have to lie to me? There *is* a child, a little boy called Jonathan, and Harry was absolutely devoted to him."

"How very touching. Probably some pauper's brat he picked up somewhere. He often affected a liking for children to impress I always suspected his many women conquests. If there is a child, very likely it is his, but it certainly is not mine."

"I simply don't believe you. The child's age is exactly right . . . almost a year, and you deserted them both because things got too difficult. How you fared between leaving them and returning home in November puzzles me. What happened to bring you to such a sorry state?"

"I have already given my explanation of that to

you and more importantly to Papa, who naturally believes my story."

"Well, I don't. I know only too well your own comfort is the most important thing in the world to you. You have taken every luxury provided as your due for years. What did you care when you broke Papa's heart? You knew only too well when you returned how soon you could wheedle your way back into the most comfortable place in the house."

"Stop talking such rubbish." Hope's voice rose hysterically. "I've had more than enough of this. How dare you question me? You are only a silly child and know nothing of life outside this smug little town."

"I have every right to question you if only for poor Harry's sake and find out what has become of the child. You must know *something*. If he were mine I would be frantic. You must help me find him."

She found herself pleading. "Please, Hope. Together we can prepare for his future."

"For Heaven's sake stop daydreaming. I tell you a child never existed. You are simply infuriated because I have not been prostrate at the murder." Hope's voice gathered momentum. "Well, I'm going to shock some sense into you. I'm glad Harry's dead, let me tell you. Glad, because now the past is over. Now I can really start living my own life again without the fear of his return ruining everything for me."

ELEVEN

SATISFACTION WAS uppermost in Matthew's mind as he sat with his port brooding over the last twenty-four hours. But relief at Mercy's report on her sister's calm acceptance of the tragedy still failed to quench an anger against the Betteridge fellow's audacity at returning to the town.

A few discreet enquiries would not come amiss, and he would make it his business to find out what really had happened. Armstrong, as the town's leading physician, would most certainly be called in for consultation. Fortunately the monthly meeting of the town's dignitaries fell on the morrow and it would not raise eyebrows to broach the subject.

What ulterior motive he wondered had brought the man back to these parts. The confidence he felt in Hope's innocence was accentuated when she appeared her usual sparkling self at supper, her manner candid and without guile.

It was not surprising that some person unknown would wish to kill the blackguard. To Matthew he was all that was despicable and, apart from the murder occurring on the brink of his own doorstep, he could not fail to feel a guilty satisfaction. The timely death had removed a stigma and certain dangerous undercurrents which might one day have erupted to the detriment of the family.

Naturally the murderer himself must be brought to justice, of this Matthew was fully aware. He himself graciously offered what facilities were available in the use of his own kitchen, for the local constable and an important Sheriff from London, working long and diligently on the case, would be in need of refreshment.

There was an unfortunate hour when the London constable called at Holly Walk. Both Matthew and Hope were absent, so Mercy was left to face the ordeal alone. She was startled and mortified to learn how much of their private affairs he knew. A hint of Hope's relations with the victim had obviously reached his ears. He was kind, however, and treated her with gentle respect, soon putting her at her ease. Mercy, almost overnight, had changed from a carefree girl into a thoughtful sensitive young woman. She felt perfectly capable of conversing intelligently and discussing whatever Mr. Whaddon chose to say to her with decorum. She answered his queries truthfully and calmly, without revealing her last meeting with Harry, offered him a glass of wine and ushered him from the house with not a little pride and satisfaction at her own conduct. She pacified Papa's indignation at what he considered the man's insolence in interviewing her, and relayed their conversation word for word over dinner.

Matthew regarded his youngest daughter reflectively and felt more than a little pleased to feel she was blossoming out so unexpectedly. It seemed she had handled the situation admirably and he was only too glad that Hope had been absent, she might have caused some harm with her unpredictable behaviour.

However, although he had agreeably accpted the men in his kitchen, the questioning of his own family he found objectionable. He would have no hesitation in taking strong action should his family be further embarrassed in spite of Mercy's protestations. It was sufficiently trying that the weekly *Courier* printed the story boldly, disclosing the gory details with gloating exultation.

Harry was buried in All Souls Churchyard, early one July morning. The use of consecrated ground was a concession granted in deference to the vicar's relationship with the deceased. The local constable escorted the body from the Assembly rooms at seven o'clock. There were no mourners.

Alfred, miserable but influenced by his strong sense of duty, committed the body to earth and the soul piously to Heaven. He was startled on lifting his eyes to notice the slight figure of Mercy standing a short distance away, head bowed in prayer as the first shower of earth fell on the coffin.

When the short service was over she laid a

bunch of fresh garden flowers on the newly dug ground and meeting her brother-in-law's gaze murmured soberly: "Who is there to cry for him? No one but me."

She continually worried about the fate of the child and racked her brains for some solution to the problem of his whereabouts. Every day, keeping her eyes and ears open for any snippet of gossip that might come her way, she visited the shops in town. The murder was naturally a source of speculation among the locals, but to her frustration the facts she gleaned were those she already knew.

There had been no further discussion between herself and Hope. Each girl preferred to avoid the other's company and she suspected Hope considered the matter closed. But Mercy had no intention of regressing and was determined to gather whatever scrap of information she could regarding the riddle of the baby. At times she felt completely lost and longed for a confidante, someone with whom to share her secret knowledge and almost unbearable suspicions, but there was no one.

She had no absolute certainty herself, only a deep unswerving belief in her own judgement, and the memory of Harry's eyes dark with tender devotion made her purpose unshakeable. Recklessly she thought of going to London and seeking out the baby herself, then dismissed the idea as impractical. Could she get away, where on earth would she start her search? All she remembered of Harry's words was Battersea. She presumed it was a district, and there was Riverside—a name he had mentioned. Was it a road, street, or walk? The connection escaped her.

She fretted for two days then decided to seek Charity's aid. Once her mind was made up she wrote a long explanatory letter and sent it direct to the hospital so that her sister would receive it without delay. Gone now was the hesitance and regret in involving the busy little nurse. That she could be relied upon Mercy was convinced. When the truth was revealed her utmost would be done to locate the child in spite of whatever commitments kept her working from dawn till dusk.

In the meantime, all she could do was wait. No further developments regarding the murder came to light and life flowed smoothly on as if nothing untoward had happened. To her surprise, Hope went several times to the Ingrams' and seemed engrossed in the business of Nancy's wedding. She discussed plans and her dress over the supper table airily, dragging Mercy reluctantly into the conversation and making Papa smile with her enthusiasm. She took over the organisation, at Nancy's request she assured them, and treated the occasion as if it were solely for her own benefit.

Matthew continued his business activities as usual. The fact that Mercy had lost some of her exuberance and looked slightly wan, puzzled him, for little escaped his sharp eyes. He wondered if perhaps she was fretting because a certain letter from India was somewhat overdue. He suggested she accompany him to Warwick but she refused and persuaded him to take Hope instead. She would be happy to supervise the house in their absence.

The day they departed Mercy anxiously watched for the afternoon post, praying a reply from Charity would conveniently arrive while she had the house to herself. Whether it was her prayers or an over-conscientious post-boy she never knew, but a familiar knock on the kitchen door sent her flying down stairs, and she almost snatched the letters from Polly's astonished hands. The maid gave a knowing little smirk as she vanished into the kitchen, believing it was the Indian postmark that had caused Miss Mercy such haste and impatience.

Of course Miles' letter was very welcome, but for once she put it aside and opened the one from Charity in the quiet of her room.

"Dearest Mercy," it ran, "I was astonished at your letter and the news it contained. What a dreadful thing to have happened to poor Mr. Betteridge. In spite of his many shortcomings there was a certain charm about him and to meet his death so horribly is a fate even the lowest villain should be spared. I prayed long and earnestly for his salvation, God rest his soul.

"The matter of the child you mention I find hard to comprehend, but if it is true that Hope is lying and behaving in the callous manner you describe, I only pray we can between us save her from any further depredation. I am doing all I can to trace any associates of Mr. Betteridge and have already sought contacts in the area you mention. It shouldn't be very difficult to find someone to bring the matter to a satisfactory conclusion. Time is the urgent factor now as it is running out fast, and I only hope I can conclude the business you require before I leave the country.

"Miss Nightingale has at last persuaded the Government to allow her a passage with a number of nuns and nurses to the Crimea, and God in His grace has granted me a place among them. If by our presence and medical skill we can bring a little comfort to the many thousands of wounded out there, any privations we may suffer ourselves will be very worthwhile.

"We sail for Scutari next month. I have written to Papa explaining the position and you can seek any further details from him. I promise you, dear Mercy, I will not leave any stone unturned to discover the child you seem certain exists and for which you feel such concern. I do trust before I leave the country all will be well, and I will contact you again whenever I have more news.

Your loving sister,
Charity."

TWELVE

THE LETTER MATTHEW received from Charity caused him some misgivings. Proud though he was that she had proved herself worthy of a place in Miss Nightingale's entourage, he had doubts about her physical ability to withstand the grim sights and arduous tasks of a field hospital.

That formidable Miss Nightingale, who had successfully formed a band of efficient nurses against inconceivable odds, was already widely known as a stoic, and would expect her followers to be likewise. Each one of her retinue would be thoroughly examined medically and theologically, and, he fully believed had Charity proved unfavourable she would have been firmly rejected. He was a little disturbed that twelve nuns would be among them. A staunch Anglican churchman himself he was highly suspicious of the Roman faith, and trusted Charity would not be influenced by their Popery.

In spite of his unease however, it was with pride that he openly boasted to his friends of his daughter's exceptional qualities.

Mercy, in spite of her disquiet regarding Harry's child and the urgency of that commission was genuinely pleased that Charity had reached her goal. The joy she must feel in spreading her knowledge and skill to such wide horizons must be very rewarding.

She enthusiastically recruited all their friends and in many a lady's sitting room an industrious circle of diligent ladies stitched strips of linen bandages and knitted helmets and mittens for the ill-clad troops. These were packed into a giant trunk with medicines and splints, candles, blankets, underwear, and a hundred and one hotch-potch articles for the war torn casualties. It was despatched by mail coach to Charity's hospital for her supervision.

In spite of all this activity the letter from Miles was primarily in Mercy's mind. He had sailed from India and would be in England by Christmas. Her joy at this alternated with tremors of misgivings. Would the dream she had cherished for so long come true, or would it vanish like the end of a rainbow? From the turmoil of her thoughts however, one thing was certain. Miles would be a rock to lean on, a haven for her worried and troubled mind. If at the end it was only friendship he offered, she knew it would be given generously and wholeheartedly.

The atmosphere between the sisters had become a little less strained. Hope began to take for granted that the animosity between them was over, and Mercy, troubled by such unease, was only too glad when her sister approached her some days before Nancy Ingram's wedding.

"Don't you think we could stop this stupidity," Hope pleaded, "and be friends again? We have scarcely spoken at all lately and I find it very depressing."

"I *should* be glad to end it, I have been unhappy too." came the impulsive reply. "But I must be honest and say I am never likely to feel quite the same towards you after the misery of the last few weeks."

"Make no mistake, my dear Mercy, I haven't forgotten the accusations you threw at me after Harry's death. Neither will I ever forgive the doubts I believe you still harbour against me.

"Don't let us discuss it any further now," Mercy begged. "Tell me a little more about Nancy's wedding; you haven't even shown me your dress. Papa says we may go to Birmingham to choose something new."

"Good. We'll go the day after tomorrow. You must have a new bonnet for the event; we'll find you something really elegant. It is high time you started to improve yourself, otherwise what will Miles think when he arrives at Christmas? Thank goodness the summer is over and we can rid you of those awful freckles; you look a real hoyden. If I mix up some cucumber and lemon cream will you promise to use it?"

Mercy nodded meekly. She quietly kept her own counsel, pleased that a more congenial atmosphere existed between them, but nevertheless not relenting an inch in her secret purpose.

They found the day they had chosen for their shopping convenient, as Papa had unexpectedly decided to go to London then, to bid Charity farewell.

The girls were faintly disturbed at being omitted, but he explained he had purposefully arranged it so. He did not wish there to be any tearful farewells, no emotional upheavals or undue stress for their sister to endure in her last hours—for God knew how long—on her native soil. As a parting gift he had purchased a mother-of-pearl prayer book locked with silver clasps, and bade them sign it lovingly.

He left before the girls were stirring and they were both soberly silent as the carriage bowled along the Birmingham road towards the shops and their busy day.

Hope's face was secretive, her thoughts reflecting perhaps on the colour of the slippers she would choose, or what wedding gift for Nancy would be most appropriate. But Mercy's were sadly on Charity and what must be her abortive attempts to trace the little lost boy, for there had been no further word from her regarding the matter. Her heart was heavy with defeat and disappointment. She felt somehow she *must* get to London herself in the near future and seek for some concrete evidence of the child's existence before the winter days made travelling impossible.

It was dusk as the girls arrived home and they

sat over a leisurely supper discussing their purchases while awaiting Matthew's return. It was late when Hope decided to retire but Mercy sat in the candlelight and bade Archer start a fire in the library, for the autumn nights were chilly and Papa would welcome the comforting glow after his long journey.

When he did arrive he was surprised to see her welcoming face and his own tired one lit up as he kissed her affectionately. Mercy noticed the lines of weariness about his mouth and realised suddenly he was ageing. There were deep wrinkles around his eyes and streaks of grey, previously unnoticed, showing as the firelight touched his thick hair. She felt a strong surge of love and loyalty sweep over her. How many fathers were so kind and considerate, so conscious of their family's welfare? Did they appreciate enough all he did for them? The diligent hours of work he consumed, the licence he allowed them, the undenied liberties granted and accepted without a second thought.

She dropped to a footstool by his feet, waiting quietly while he ate the light meal Archer provided. When he settled relaxed, contented with a glass of his favourite brandy, she coaxed him to tell her about his day.

"Ah, Mercy. It is good to be home," he sighed. "London is a wonderful place but has more lonely souls I do believe that the whole of England put together, but Charity was not in the least dejected; she was as happy and excited as I ever recollect seeing her over the prospect of this venture.

"I fear a little for Charity though; she looks so frail. Many of her fellow nurses are as strong and healthy as our local country girls, but your sister's strength is in the heart. God grant it will protect and sustain her through this disastrous campaign."

They sat silent for a while and as Mercy rose to leave her father produced two envelopes from his pocket.

"Charity handed me a letter for each of you, just a farewell message I presume. Goodnight my dear, sleep well."

In her room with impatient fingers Mercy opened the letter. Charity had wasted no time in fripperies and commenced immediately with the news she longed to hear.

" . . . the address is as follows," Here, a house in Battersea—Riverside Crescent—was mentioned.

"When I received the satisfactory information I went myself to deal with it. It is as you expected, there *is* a child. He is fifteen months old and the loveliest little boy imaginable. If there was a doubt in my mind of his parentage there is none now, for he is the exact image of his mother. Take a look at the miniature of Hope at that age, on the drawing-room piano, and you will be looking at Jonathan. The same bright blue eyes and yellow curls, even the dimple in his chin is there. Hope's attitude is quite beyond comprehension and if you can persuade her yourself to pay him a visit she cannot fail to respond to his appeal. Have no fears for his welfare; he is being cared for by a kind motherly soul called Mrs. Boniface. I made myself known, telling her I was a relative of the child's dead father. She was very distressed about the tragedy, and told me the police had questioned her. I do not think she told them the child was Harry's. She seems devoted to him and even at her own expense was determined no harm should come to the little one. She is a seamstress and works exclusively for wealthy influential ladies, so has ample provisions. I have however arranged with a doctor at the hospital for her to receive a small stipend each month towards the child's keep. He has of course agreed to treat the affair with strict confidence, although during the last few days I have noticed an odd curiosity in the looks he bestows upon me . . ." Mercy smiled to herself, visualising the twinkle in Charity's eyes as she wrote this. "Mrs. Boniface," the letter went on, "is reasonably educated so will be able to reply to your correspondence if you can find some means of communicating. It is with deepest satisfaction, dearest Mercy, I am able to relieve your mind of anxiety before embarking on my expedition abroad . . ."

The letter went on to express concern for Hope's salvation and made reference to the coming months and partaking of God's work in a strange and frightening country.

Mercy sat for some time with the paper in her hands while the night crept on. It was early morning before she lay down to sleep, happier and with a lighter heart than for some time gone. Her sleep was deep and sound, and she dreamed of Miles and a new life spreading before her, fresh, simple, and with the past nightmare of confusion gone.

It had unfortunately rained continually for three days before Nancy's wedding, and her father's farm at Radford Semele was awash. Hope wrinkled her nose at the smell from the cowsheds and remarked that Nancy had, considering her background, done remarkably well for herself. The family she had married into were county folk and reasonably well off, the young couple setting up house in a sizeable establishment in Clarendon Square. Although, Hope remarked acidly, to hear the bride one would think it was Warwick Castle itself!

After that, it seemed too soon winter was upon them. November brought its usual dripping trees, and fog around the river. It was damp and mild as the month drew to its close.

There had been no news from Charity, but word that Miss Nightingale's party had on November 5th arrived safely in Scutari was reported in the papers. It was understood conditions were appaling. Further than that no details were published and it was left for anxious families to wait as patiently as possible for private letters to reach them. The Prime Minister felt the situation was being exaggerated and expressed his disapproval once again of the permission granted to women being allowed on the battle front. He considered them most unsuitable subjects for such a venture.

The family felt extreme alarm when Charity's

THE HOUSE IN HOLLY WALK

letters *did* begin to arrive. She sent news of unspeakable battles. Balaclava, with the Light Infantry cut to pieces ending in deplorable loss of life, horrified them all. It had taken days to get the wounded across the Bosporus to the Barracks Hospital where they were received in indescribable conditions. They guessed by her writing the effort it must have cost her weary hand to hold the pen whilst dropping with fatigue. But they little knew there was scarcely a bed for her to rest on had there been time to lay her aching body down. Her life, and that of her companions was one continual round of horror. Dressing gangrenous wounds, supporting fever-stricken heads, hiding fearful eyes while a limb was amputated without anaesthetic. Writing a man's last letter home, clearing up blood, vomit and lice. Dragging their skirts among the filth of a plasma strewn floor, and toiling ceaselessly, hour after nightmare hour to produce out of the general chaos some semblance of order and cleanliness. Their own fatigue must be kept from the wounded men's eyes; the nurses were expected to show a quiet serenity, to carry peace and tranquillity to the very gates of hell.

Meanwhile nothing had transpired from the constable's investigations into the murder case and Mr. Whaddon had returned to London. He assured the dignitaries of the town however the affair would not be forgotten, but filed away in London's City Hall, for revision when the necessity arose.

Christmas was a busy time for the Church and Faith was bearing her third pregnancy remarkably well, but Alfred was grateful that both his sisters-in-law offered to decorate his own church of All Souls.

A little ashamed at her own deceit, Mercy had found a way of communicating with Mrs. Boniface in Battersea. The posting coach left town once a week for London, and the Cockney driver, unaware of Mercy's identity, was only too pleased to carry letters back and forth for the ladylike young miss prepared to pay him a florin each time for his trouble.

Although illspelt and grammatically erroneous, the letters Mercy received from Mrs. Boniface were explicit and heart-warming, and she felt until other arrangements could be made they would suffice. Everything centred now on Miles' homecoming, and as Christmas week approached Mercy, bemused, had but one thought in her mind echoing repeatedly the whispered words, "I shall come back for you."

To Matthew, Christmas had always been a magical time of goodwill and holly and bells. He was determined that despite Charity's absence the season should be a merry one.

Chafing a little about the lack of male company, he allowed Hope to invite the newly married Nancy and a party of young people staying in their house.

"I can't say there is anyone particularly suitable," Hope gloomily confided to Mercy.

THE HOUSE IN HOLLY WALK

"Suitable for whom?" came the innocent reply.

"You know what I mean," Hope returned, flushing a little. "We are so short of eligible men, and I've yet to meet one to impress me."

"Well, perhaps you will among the Adler's friends. I do believe you are looking for a husband." This teasing came from Faith, who with her children was taking tea at Holly Walk.

The other tossed her head but Faith looked at her quizzically, guessing how often she must yearn for male companionship. But with all her trials and experiences, nothing seemed to affect Hope's beauty or dim her brilliant eyes.

With what nervous anticipation Mercy awaited Miles' arrival; the sound of horses' hooves on the sparkling gravel or a sharp knock on the front door seemed to stop her heart beating.

Boxing day was upon them and the house glowed with light. Bright fires blazed in every room and these were more than welcome as the guests began to arrive, for a hard sharp frost and a full moon turned the skeleton trees to silver.

Hope, a vision in pink and white, mingled with the younger guests and started the dancing with the handsomest man in sight. Matthew smiled indulgently, hoping perhaps a little wistfully there might be a future blossoming for her, for several of the young men were extremely presentable. He looked around for Mercy and saw her descending the stairs, resplendent in a new white crinoline trimmed with hyacinth blue ribbons the colour of her eyes. Her chestnut hair, in spite of vigorous brushing tumbled about her shoulders. Even as the astonishing thought struck him of how beautiful she had become, a thunderous knocking on the front door sent Archer swiftly running.

There stood Miles, resplendent in his scarlet cloak, dark handsome eyes sparkling with pleasure.

As he stepped into the hall dozens of eyes watched, and all conversation flagged. The orchestra tinkled away thinly in the background as Matthew came forward smiling.

But Miles looked to the stairs where the tremulous figure of Mercy stood, flushed and covered with confusion. He had eyes for no one but her, and he strode across and lifted her bodily down. He took both her hands before the astonished crowd and gazed into her eyes. A breathless stillness encompassed them both.

"I told you I would return," he whispered softly.

The spell was broken. Matthew grasped the outstretched hand. Hope, hovering with excitement, was waiting to be introduced, and a general babble of talk burst forth. There were twitterings of surprise and slight palpitations from some of the elder ladies, and booms of welcoming laughter came with witty remarks from the gentlemen. To add to the confusion, Gyp bounded up the kitchen stairs yelping in a frenzy of ecstasy. He wasn't one to forget an old friend, as Mercy explained.

The dancing was soon in full swing once more, and at the hub, a bright jacket and a froth of white petticoats whirled in unison. Chattering, laughing, making up in the space of minutes time that in long weary wasted months now was forgotten.

Hope watched them, vivaciously gay and perhaps a little effusive with one of her new male friends. But her eyes were shadowed and dark with envious longing. She, who had so often been the belle of the ball, was now outshone by a peculiar glow of happiness surrounding the united couple.

When time was taken out for refreshment, everyone flocked around Miles. He brought entertaining news of Aunt Lydia and her exciting life in India. He answered questions for the benefit of the gentlemen on the far East situation, taking care not to alarm the ladies. He courteously seated the pregnant Faith, enquiring after Alfred and her family, and listened attentively to the story of Charity's rewarding work. He waited with deference on Hope, amused at her flirtatious eyes, but always at his side was Mercy, her little hand tucked protectively beneath his arm, his secret smiling glances only for her.

Later, when the party was over and guests gone, he sat with Matthew over port and cigars and wasted no time.

"I feel this opportunity has been sent for a purpose, sir. As you know my service in India was scheduled for five years, but now the situation has changed.

"You must have known with what esteem I held Mercy even before I left, but I had no idea myself how much I would miss her or how very much she meant to me until the long months apart seemed endless. My letters have naturally had to be restrained as I could not declare my feelings or expect her youth to be wasted waiting, perhaps years, for my return. Now the matter is very different and I am requesting your support, and I hope your blessing, in considering your daughter as my wife."

Although expecting this declaration, Matthew compromised.

"I know that Mercy has heard from you regularly and it is not my custom to pry into my family's correspondence. She has naturally always received your letters with pleasure and has made little secrecy of their contents. Indeed, quite often we have been entertained over the breakfast table by extracts from their interesting news. It is not my place to express an opinion on her regard for you, but I must say on receiving word of your homecoming she has been extremely happy."

"Then you have no objection to my approaching her?"

Matthew drew slowly on his cigar.

"The only objection I can raise is this Crimean business. How long do you think it will last, and how great the danger? I take it you will be involved in serious fighting?"

"It depends partly on Sardinia and if they join us in quelling the Russians. You will I am sure appreciate I have no choice but to do my duty to my country, as every Englishman expects a man of my profession to do."

"My dear boy, of course I understand and I appreciate your patriotic feelings. But Mercy's happiness is very dear to me and the risk of her being widowed at such an early age appalls me."

"I can understand that. But now that we have really found each other I simply cannot bear losing her again, whatever the odds may be. I feel she will think as I do and we would not wish to wait. Providing she will accept me, I would want us to be married at once in spite of her being so young."

"You forget she is now over nineteen years and although in many ways still a child at heart, she has taken over and performed very proficiently many of the duties Charity left to her. Although she has led a comparatively sheltered life we have had our own tragedies here, as you will probably soon learn from Mercy herself. These things have done much to develop her character and she is quite capable of withstanding a great deal."

"Then I have your consent, sir?"

"Yes, you have my consent, Miles, and also my blessing. The only sorrow I feel will be when you return from this unpleasant war you will take away another of my daughters. I presume Mercy's life as an officer's wife will follow the pattern of her Aunt Lydia's and she will be continually travelling to distant places. Be that as it may. Good luck, my boy, and God bless you."

Raising their glasses, the men drank to each other with mutual respect.

After the younger man had left, Matthew sat

morosely in thought. How much better fitted for the wandering Army man's life would Hope have been. If only she, restless, still unpredictable, could find someone as responsible as Miles to cherish her and give her all the excitement her dissatisfied heart craved.

The influx of visitors in the house made it difficult for the lovers to snatch a few minutes alone, but the next day, when a pale wintry sun flickered feebly before setting, Miles looked out onto the sparkling frost and suggested they take a walk. Mercy's eyes shone and whistling Gyp they set off briskly until the colour in Mercy's cheeks was almost as gay as the ribbons on her Christmas bonnet. Miles laughed with pleasure as he looked at her.

"Oh, my darling Mercy, what a joy you are to behold. I don't need to tell you why I am here, do I?"

She shook her head, her heart too full to speak.

"I have spoken with your father, and he has given his consent. May I now seek it from you, my dearest?"

"Oh you know it. All along you have known, ever since our last meeting. Why did you wait so long before telling me?"

"I love you, Mercy. I am telling you now. I yearned to write it in every letter, but how could I with the future so uncertain and our next meeting perhaps years away."

"All those letters wasted, when I longed so much to see the words before me. I felt I couldn't bear it."

Smiling, he took her face between his hands lovingly.

"That's what I like best about you, Mercy: you are so refreshing and honest. No false swooning or sly surprise about you."

"You surely don't think I am too forward, do you?" she asked anxiously.

"Forward enough to name the day. When will you marry me?"

"Soon. As soon as you wish."

"The quicker the better. We have wasted enough time already and remember I have only a month before we shall be parting again for a while."

She shivered. "Oh, Miles. That horrible war."

He stopped her frightened shaking voice as he bent to kiss the ready lips beneath his own. She thrust unwelcome thoughts away and her heart overflowed with longing.

Arms entwined they wandered, oblivious of the fading light until frost sparkling on his moustache made Mercy giggle with delight. Eagerly they made their plans between sweet murmured nothings, folded around by wings of love.

THIRTEEN

NEVER HAD A wedding caused such a flutter among the female society of the town. Everyone was wholly elated with the affair, for Mercy herself was much liked in the community and a favourite with all. Her bright face bent to anyone in trouble endeared her to many. Everyone wished her well and, despite some speculation among the dowagers at the swift arrangements, no one openly criticised Matthew for allowing the hurried marriage.

There was a frenzy of organisation below stairs. The whole staff was determined Miss Mercy's day should, in spite of such short notice, be as grand and successful as Miss Faith's had been two years previously. Cook worked unceasingly, planning with Hope, who did her best, but found it difficult to concentrate on such mundane things as food when the more exciting event of the bride's trousseau had to be so speedily arranged. The feeling of envy and resentfulness at her sister's good fortune she succeeded in concealing very well, and the lists of guests she compiled grew with such alacrity that Mercy became alarmed. Both she and Miles wished for a quiet affair, and in the end she had no alternative but to beg her father to curb Hope's enthusiasm. Miles had persuaded Matthew to allow the wedding to take place exactly ten days after the engagement was announced. The remaining two weeks of his leave must be spent alone with his bride before the inevitable farewell.

The day was set for January 7th and everyone hoped the bright frosty weather would continue.

"A bride could look enchanting in scarlet velvet with white fur, against a snowy background," suggested Hope optimistically.

"And would then need a beard to be turned into St. Nicholas," laughed Mercy. "No thank you, do please let me design my own wedding gown."

Hope shook her head resignedly.

"Well choose something suitable. Miles is an extremely handsome man and you must do him justice."

The local seamstress was immediately engaged and enrolled the help of several colleagues to stitch far into the night preparing Mercy's trousseau. The wedding gown was this lady's own undertaking, sewing every stitch herself, for she had dressed the bride from childhood. The lilac velvet Mercy chose was to be simple and feminine with no bows and unnecessary frills. Matthew himself, now resigned to the idea that the small local shops no longer satisfied his family, had sought out the material himself in Birmingham and treated her to enough ermine for a warm attractive muff. The matching bonnet was also trimmed with this luxurious and expensive fur.

Hope battled with the bride's uncontrollable hair, trying to coax it into shape, but its natural buoyancy refused to settle into the now fashionable corkscrew curls.

To complicate matters, in the midst of the preparations a cry for help came from Charity. Equipment and medicines, particularly bandages and drugs, were desperately needed on the war front and would Papa please organise whatever supplies he could at the first opportunity. No pittance was too small and the despairing cry written so starkly, brought home to them all how frightening must be the carnage of the battlefields.

Matthew, with Miles, who snatched a precious day away from his bride-to-be, took a train to London and together assembled a dozen large trunks, seeing that preferential treatment was awarded them. With a bribe of several sovereigns immediate delivery to the docks was assured.

When they returned, harassed and disconsolate at what they considered to be a drop in the ocean for humanity, Mercy met them her face troubled. The urgency and futile waste of war was uppermost in her mind and she was remorseful at the money being spent on the luxury of her own wedding while such pitiable hardships abounded elsewhere.

"It is no good fretting, darling," Miles comforted her. "A soldier's life is made of unrest. The thing that offends me most is the intolerance of the Government. Let the struggle continue to the bitter end providing it is not on British soil. From thousands of miles away the smell of blood cannot disturb their complacency. Oh they give their gold generously enough and then sit back smugly satisfied they have done their bit. But the funds are badly mismanaged and will be fostered greedily until too late. The money should be *spent now* for clothing and arms and better food for the troops. There have always been cruel battles fought in the name of England, for the glory of its name and the Captain's pride, but how many have given a thought to the plight of the common soldier, uncouth, illiterate, bowed under discipline? Fighting, suffering without question and dying ignorantly for a cause which to him has no end."

A compassionate officer with such sincere humanity was unique in a time when flesh and blood was cheap and a man's life could be thrown away carelessly to further a superior's cause. Mercy realised how eternally grateful she would always be for so merciful a man, but the thought of his immediate future in the bloodbath of the Crimea tormented her.

Miles dismissed such gloomy subjects and spoke of his desire to take Mercy away for at least a week. Would she care for the sea, or would the idea of London appeal to her?

London. Mercy's heart leapt. She had found no opportunity to discuss the problem of Hope's child with him. She had decided to keep it to herself a little longer, and during the long intimate hours of their honeymoon now thankfully she would pour out her troubled secrets. If they were to be wholly one, the lightening of each other's load must be shared and in their quiet moments she could tell him of the baby. While in London he would help her seek him out and put to rest the unreasonable half fears that still persisted until she had seen with her own eyes all was well. Miles would advise her wisely and show her how to react should Hope still insist in the emphatic denial of her son.

When Mercy looked back on her wedding and the following days in London it was a dream of delight. Every detail was engraved upon her heart.

The day itself with a sprinkling of featherlight snow, the warmth of her family and friends shone like a beacon among her souvenirs.

From Gloucester, Miles' father, whose twinkling eyes gave lie to his stern expression, with the flutter of Mercy's new sisters-in-law were lodged in the small but respectable Clarendon Hotel. Her mother-in-law's health was too delicate to endure the tiring journey.

She would always recall Alfred's solemn face as he conducted the marriage service and the hushed congregation smiling when the crescendo of wedding music swept them from the freezing church. Perhaps most of all would she remember coming out into the dazzling light with her tall husband by her side, the gold braid of his uniform outshining the sudden winter sun, the plume of green feathers in his shako dancing in the wind.

London and its gaiety in the new year was infectious. Their hotel was the height of fashionable splendour. Huge crystal chandeliers sparkled lavishly even in broad daylight, and the whisper of expensive skirts and the waft of subtle perfume were extravagantly apparent. The confusion Mercy felt when first being addressed as Mrs. Finch brought a grin of pleasure from Miles.

In the privacy of their room, her trembling nervousness was unfounded. Her new husband, however travelled and hardened a soldier he might be, treated his bride as tenderly as one would a butterfly, careful not to bruise her wings. With gentle coaxing he smoothed her fright, although loving her ardently enough to evoke her natural instincts and bring to their first days together a level of enchantment. It was a time for Mercy to remember after he had gone, a wistful halcyon dream.

They drove into Hyde Park and watched the riders in Rotten Row, and brought flowers and heather for luck from the sellers in Piccadilly. They walked boldly by the fast-flowing river, ignoring the newsboys' yells of gloomy war campaigns while the east wind brought a glow to their faces.

Miles insisted on showering her with gifts. The most precious possession he gave her was a little Swiss music box, beautifully enamelled and tinkling away a merry tune. She was to play it with nostalgia in the lonely weeks ahead.

When she told Miles, now without restraint,

about Hope's baby, he listened attentively and promised they should take a cab the next morning and seek out the house in Battersea.

It was perfectly simple. The house, in a neat little red brick terrace, prim with spotless lace curtains, was easily located and Mrs. Boniface all that Charity had foretold. She welcomed them, busily putting on a kettle for tea while they played with the little boy. Like any child being the centre of attention, he laughed and showed his little white teeth delightedly.

"He *is* like Hope. Don't you agree?" whispered Mercy happily. "There cannot be any mistake, and yet the turn of his head is unmistakenly Harry's. Oh how can she be so unfeeling? If only we could take him home."

Miles ignored this suggestion as premature but was pleased for his wife's sake the child's welfare was established. He pressed ten shining guineas into the reluctant hand of the seamstress, with promises of future contacts, and as they drove back to their hotel he suggested Mercy dismiss the episode. Now they must concentrate on their next few days together; she must trust him, for any complications that arose could be dealt with satisfactorily.

She felt tears of relief and happiness behind her eyes and was now prepared to enjoy every single minute of their time together.

On returning to Holly Walk their first days were filled with social engagements. Everyone wished for their company and time spent with friends seemed to snatch the days away, and she knew the hours she and Miles had left were rapidly diminishing.

Matthew had thoughtfully arranged that Charity's old room be decorated and furnished as a private sitting-room for the newly-weds. He wished to allow them as much time alone as possible. He even had the green-painted spinet which was his own pride and joy removed into their quarters where Miles, an accomplished player, could entertain his bride.

There was so much Mercy had yet to learn about her new husband. The fact that he, superb soldier and a fine horseman, should perform with so delicate a touch on the little French instrument astonished her. After supper they retired to this welcoming sanctuary from well-meaning friends and the prying eyes of Hope. She herself, never having known jealousy, was amused at Hope's coquetry towards Miles. She monopolised the conversation at meals, appeared in her most becoming gowns, and laughed so vivaciously that even Matthew frowned disapprovingly at her unseemly behaviour.

Then one dreary dark February morning Miles was gone. He and Mercy talked far into the night, determined to look forward and plan for the future. But a hundred and one things were left unsaid and swiftly the hours passed until Mercy sat at her window, exhaustion on her tear-stained face, watching the carriage roll out of the drive.

The future months of waiting were going to seem like years.

FOURTEEN

MATTHEW WAS CONFINED to the house with a severe cold. He, whose health was usually so hearty, remained in bed during the first feverish days, a comforting bright fire burning in his room. He insisted however to Hope's disapproval in having the windows thrown wide.

Archer was an excellent nurse and treated the invalid with firm but attentive care. Matthew admittedly was a little sick of female company. Hope's mouth seemed set these days in a continual pout of boredom and discontent, and when she asked prmission to go to Cambridge for a while with the Adlers and a party of friends, he felt nothing but relief. Mercy he could tolerate. She still spent much time out of doors and whatever the weather could be found, sometimes riding her cob across the open countryside but more often with Gyp, idling through the tree-lined lanes. Her attention was inclined to wander frequently, but she was back at Holly Walk in time for the postman's knock, her eager hands searching the mail. If there was a letter from Miles she would read it repeatedly. Often Matthew had seen the candle burning late at night in her sitting-room where a plaintive tune from the tinkling little music box could be faintly heard bringing her comfort.

Hope had been gone three days when a large trunk arrived from Aunt Lydia containing presents for them all and late wedding gifts for Mercy. There was a beautiful Kashmir shawl which she draped artistically over the spinet in her sitting-room, for Papa had allowed her to retain the little instrument indefinitely.

The letter accompanying the gift was long and affectionate. That her aunt was gratified at the marriage was obvious. She wrote enthusiastically of welcoming Mercy with her husband to India when this present wretched war was over and Miles would again take up his duties in the East.

Mercy sat before the half-opened box thinking of Miles and wondering wistfully how long it would be before she could expect to receive regular letters from him. There had been only two so far. One, short but loving, convincing her of his safe arrival in the Crimea. The other from a place called Sevastopol. It was absurd, she realised, to hope he would make any contact with Charity in Scutari, but this unlikely event crossed her mind repeatedly bringing a small comfort.

That there had been no fruitful conclusion from the exquisite nights of love shared so briefly on that idyllic honeymoon was to her a bitter disappointment. She had prayed so earnestly for a child to ease the lonely ache in her heart during the long empty months ahead.

Matthew was beginning to convalesce and doing so with a bad grace. He had developed a troublesome cough which prevented him from enjoying his favourite cigars, and from attending his office. He prowled about the house in an old velvet smoking jacket, and found no pleasure in prized familiar things, nor anything to please him in his comfortable surroundings.

A sombre letter from Charity did little to improve his state of mind. Owing to a breakdown of communications and disgraceful bungling on the part of the War Office, the supplies sent by himself and many other organisations had failed to arrive at their destination. Possibly they lay with countless others, rotting under snow at Balaclava, or hidden by refuse in some far distant customs house.

Whatever the cause, hideously wounded men were denied the comforts despatched from England and Charity bitterly reproached the administration in the sparse heartbreaking lines she wrote. That she kept much to herself Matthew was aware as she always ended on a cheerful note, believing implicitly that God would bring a better tomorrow. Matthew's own methods of obtaining news however did nothing to ease his fears. Terrifying stories of cholera ravaging the troops and medical staff alike reached his ears. This he hid from the girls, but the dread concern he felt for his

THE HOUSE IN HOLLY WALK

brave far-distant daughter only aggravated further his flagging spirits.

A sudden bombshell came however which shook him out of his lethargy.

Carriage wheels in the drive one afternoon led Mercy to believe Hope had arrived home in the railroad hackney, but glancing out of the drawing-room window she was surprised to see a smart phaeton drawn by two high-stepping greys, halt outside the door. Down stepped Hope, in her smartest outfit, accompanied by a broad-shouldered man of medium height resplendent in a grey morning suit and the newest shining top hat.

Hastily smoothing her dimity skirt Mercy came down stairs to find Papa had forestalled her and stood in the hall while Archer opened the door.

Hope entered gaily, her light laughter and effervescent spirit already filling the house.

"Dear Papa, are you feeling better? I must say you look greatly improved since I saw you last. It is nice to be home."

She stood on her toes to kiss her father's cheek, and Mercy's perceptive nature became acutely aware of a certain nervous tension in her manner. She was wryly conscious in that fleeting moment of how distrustful she had become of all this sister's actions.

Hope drew her companion forward boldly. The disclosure she made was brutally frank.

"I have a surprise for you both. This is my husband, Paul Cohen. We were married in Cambridge yesterday."

Mercy saw her father's face, still pale from his illness turn a little more grey and the shoulders sag. Her eyes willed his to meet her own. She was soundlessly giving him courage, entreating him to face with dignity this unpardonable act.

To her relief he straightened his back and when he spoke his voice was smooth, without emotion.

"A surprise indeed, Hope. Come into the Library where we can talk." He dismissed Archer with a nod and led the little party into the inner sanctum, firmly closing the door.

The younger man brought forward a chair and removing Hope's wrap, laid his own hat on the leather-topped table. Whilst Papa silently produced glasses and his best Madeira, Mercy looked swiftly at the man Hope had married. She judged him to be in his middle thirties with intent dark eyes and a pleasant smile, but there was something familiar about him which puzzled her.

Papa's hand pouring the wine was quite steady and his voice when he spoke deceptively mild.

"Surely there is no need for you to look so uncommonly nervous, my dear," he remarked, looking at his wilful daughter.

Hope flushed and spoke rapidly.

"Well, you see, Papa, I was a little uncertain about how you would receive the news. I did not wish to distress you unduly, but when you have heard the facts I am sure you will understand."

"I hope so. Was the unseemly haste really necessary? Could you not have brought your gentleman friend home and sought my consent as is the usual custom, or am I such a tyrant as to make that impossible?"

"Not at all, Papa. In fact Paul was very anxious it should be done in the proper manner, but I wasn't prepared for it. I refused to consider being married by Alfred with all the fuss of another wedding at All Souls. Isn't it enough that Faith and Mercy were married there conventionally without myself conforming too?"

"Each must have a choice I agree, but the courtesy of first presenting your intended husband to me would, I feel, have been more considerate."

The other man prepared to speak, but Hope silenced him with a gesture.

"Had you been a little more perceptive, Papa, you would have realised that Paul has been a guest in our house several times. He was groomsman to Percy when he married Nancy and was present at our own New Year's party."

This instantly explained his familiarity to Mercy. But how was she expected to remember anything of that unforgettable night when Miles arrived from India. She felt at the moment uncomfortably obtuse, and knew that she should make some comment, but before she could do so her father spoke again, not to his daughter but directly to the man at her side.

"As you are my daughter's husband and she has been so remiss, perhaps you will be good enough to disclose something of your background, sir. I believe Cohen was the name she used. Surely that is Jewish?"

The swarthy appearance and distinctly prominent nose certainly pointed to those origins, but the man smilingly shook his head.

"There were former connections years ago, but neither I nor my family are orthodox Jews. I realise, my dear sir, the shock you must feel, and please believe me when I say it was not our wish to cause you distress. I have been deeply attached to your daughter for some months, but it wasn't until we arrived in Cambridge that our feelings overcame us. We were married in a beautiful chapel, one which my friends and I hold in deep esteem. Most of us when students in that city used to attend services there and somehow the opportunity was perfect. Do please forgive the impetuosity; we had not the will to reject it. The chance of a gathering of old friends in such circumstances seemed unlikely to occur again, and our love and enthusiasm got the better of us."

His cultured voice and impeccable manner was impressive and Mercy, stealing a look at her father, broke in.

"I feel, Papa, we should allow Hope and Mr. Cohen a little relaxation and some refreshment before any further discussion. Suppose I arrange supper early. It will give us all time to recover."

Matthew assented, with she sensed a certain amount of relief. What he felt as the two mounted the stairs his controlled manner succeeded in hiding.

She suggested in a whispered aside to Hope they use her own sitting-room until other arrangements could be made.

At the supper table, hastily relaid for four, a more relaxed air did little to quell a certain uneasiness on the part of both girls.

Hope, refusing to admit any guilt but worried nevertheless at her own daring, was unnaturally subdued, cautiously letting the men converse, and obviously wishing her husband to shoulder the responsibility for their disparaging behaviour.

Mercy, troubled for her father still recuperating from his illness, studied the inscrutable face. The astounding news he had received must be causing him untold anguish, but he ignored the subject of their marriage and questioned the other man about his interests, prospects and ability. The answers he received were open enough. His father owned a flourishing draper's business in Bristol and was wealthy enough to support his only son substantially, but Paul had no head for business and had, from his student days, been interested in journalism. On leaving Cambridge he had, with his own skill and ingenuity, become well known in literary circles. Now part of the complicated machinery of supplying news on a variety of events to the public, he was employed by a discerning and very respectable daily newspaper.

Hope, sensing her father's interest, and seeing he was not unimpressed, shed her acquired meekness and addressed him proudly.

"You will understand about our hasty marriage, Papa, when I tell you Paul has at last realised his ambition and is being sent to Turkey by his newspaper as a war correspondent. He is replacing a colleague unfortunately wounded out there. I am afraid he has to leave very shortly, within a few days in fact."

Matthew murmured commiserations, then turned to the younger man.

"A very gratifying assignment, Mr. Cohen, but a dangerous mission no doubt. I believe reports sent by Mr. Russell are scandalising the Government and indeed terrifying the public by their shocking accounts."

"Oh Papa, please call him Paul. After all he is one of the family now."

"Very well, if it pleases you. But if we are to consider ... er ... Paul one of the family, I conclude he will know all our family secrets. Have *all* the skeletons come out of the cupboard, Hope?"

The girl drew in her breath sharply and Mercy felt her stomach flutter with nerves as she looked at her father's face, Mr. Cohen, wiping his moustache with his napkin, looked Matthew squarely in the eyes.

"I understand, sir, that my wife travelled abroad for a year or so with companions, and I trust I am broad-minded enough to realise that a foreign country may lead to a few indiscretions. I hope I have enough foresight to feel a woman should have certain privileges, within reason naturally. But Hope has told me her upbringing has been conducted by a very enlightened and modern father and I don't think we have kept any secrets from each other. Now I have met you, sir, and can appreciate your qualities, I am sure in spite of your advanced views you would never allow scandal to circulate, or irregular conduct to involve any of your daughters. You need have no fear, I am sure there is little about Hope I do not already know."

Hope's face was deathly white and almost panic stricken. Instinctively Mercy realised he was totally ignorant of her past. What would Papa do? His manner gave no indication and she herself felt a strong desire to run from the table before the tense atmosphere exploded about them. If there was to be a scene, cowardly as it might be, she wanted no part of it. There were enough problems already and she must remove herself and inevitably Hope from further embarrassment. Whatever dilemma arose, let the gentlemen settle it in private.

She rose and looked across at her sister.

"You look pale, Hope. I think the journey and excitement has been too much for you."

She stretched out her hand and Hope, her mouth set with fear, clutched it gratefully.

"Will you excuse us please. After a short rest I am sure she will be perfectly all right," Mercy assured the concerned husband.

Together they left the room, but the look of appeal Hope shot her father was beseeching.

Upstairs in the drawing-room Mercy produced a glass of port for her sister and watched the colour flow back into her face.

"You are a fool, Hope," she reproached angrily. "Do you really mean to say you married Mr. Cohen keeping him in ignorance of all that has happened? No wonder it was all done so secretly!"

"Don't keep calling him Mr. Cohen, his name's Paul and he is my husband. Nothing can alter that. I told him of my year abroad . . . ."

"But not with whom you spent it!"

"Am I never to be allowed to forget that? Paul wanted me for his wife so why should I jeopardise both his and my own happiness. He is not a raw young subaltern you know, but a sophisticated man of the world, and what I failed to tell him he probably guessed. Anyway at the appropriate time I shall be quite prepared to explain everything, that is if Papa does not take it upon himself to ruin it all. If he attempts to poison Paul's mind against me I shall never forgive him as long as I live."

"You can hardly expect everyone to fall in with your plans and ignore your former behaviour. But Papa will be obliged to treat the matter as impartially as possible out of respect for the family."

Behind the defiant eyes Mercy saw naked fear. She forced herself to ask the question uppermost in her mind."

"And what about your child?"

"Oh for Heaven's sake, Mercy, you are still not harping on that old story. How many times do I have to deny it?" She dismissed the subject with a shrug, and said: "I wonder what is keeping them so long."

Mercy felt disturbed at her own lack of sympathy, for the pathetic attempt of indifference did not deceive her. She knew how agonisingly Hope was awaiting the outcome of the interview between her husband and father. She also realised how unfeeling she herself was growing, but her sister's uncontrolled wilfulness had done enough damage already in this house, and she stifled an impulse to comfort as the other began to pace the room.

It seemed like hours before they heard footsteps on the stairs and the two men entered.

The younger one came directly to his bride and ignoring her anxiety took her hands. Almost at once a courteous goodnight to the others was made and as they left the room Mercy glanced enquiringly at her father.

Matthew stood with his back to the fire, looking sharply round the room. He strode to replace a spray of lilac fallen from its bowl and suddenly Mercy felt immensely elated, with an overwhelming desire to laugh. Without warning or a period of transition, Papa was well again. Alert, critical and controlled in the old familiar way, he smiled at her affectionately.

"Well, my dear, so another of my daughters is now a married woman. I think Hope has at least realised life is not one continual bed of roses and has shown enough good sense to find herself a very astute husband. Paul Cohen seems a remarkable man, and if I am any judge will certainly one day make an impact on the literary world. He tells me he is engaged in writing a thesis, a historical work on the life and times of George I. What a pity it has to be interrupted by the war as some further research he was contemplating must wait until his return. He has however done me the honour of offering the incomplete manuscript for my perusal, a gesture I greatly appreciate."

Speechless, Mercy waited as he went on.

"Knowing how fond you are of reading I think you may be allowed to look, providing Hope agrees of course."

"I would like that." She paused. "Papa, what about Hope? What did you discuss with her husband? The atmosphere when we left seemed very unpredictable."

"To be truthful with you, Mercy, I was almost at a loss. I felt no honourable man should be deceived by a snippet of a girl, and that the culprit is my own daughter causes me much aggravation. However, I weighed the question in my mind and decided the question of her past is better left dormant. Hope has changed somewhat since that escapade; I earnestly believe she is remorseful and will make a good and excellent wife. Her pleasures have been comparatively few lately, and to my mind she has now suffered enough. Marrying this man—although I do not condone the way it was done; I shall severely reprimand her on that—will I think be her salvation. He is no love-stricken boy, but a man of ability and experience and on the whole I feel she has been extraordinarily fortunate to have done so well. No, my dear, revealing the past will only cause unnecessary pain. They are married now and I trust all will go well with them. Just as yourself and Miles had but a few short days together, so is the case with then. They must be left in peace to enjoy them."

FIFTEEN

PLEASED AS SHE was at the outcome of Hope's latest escapade, Mercy spent a restless night. She liked Mr. Cohen, he had apparently impressed Matthew and she agreed with her father's words, that the marriage might be the making of Hope. How happy she would have been for them if only the knowledge of the little boy in London did not haunt her so. Earlier in the evening, when Hope's deceit had angered her, she had decided to reveal everything to her father. But how could she now completely ruin her sister's chances of happiness? Perhaps if she herself were more tolerant and understanding she might one day persuade Hope to confess the whole sad story herself, but until that day it must be locked away in the quiet corners of her mind.

Towards dawn she fell into an uneasy sleep to be awakened it seemed instantaneously by a thunderous knocking on the front door. Dazed, she leapt out of the bed and ran into the corridor, where she saw Papa ahead of her running down the stairs. Archer was up from the basement before them, thin legs emerging bare from his voluminous nightshirt. He flung open the door to admit Alfred, gasping for breath, his face dripping with perspiration.

"The child is coming and Faith is in terrible pain. The midwife's with her, and Betty, but she is calling for Mercy and I must get Dr. Armstrong."

Matthew took complete control, ordering Archer to saddle the cob, and Mercy flew to dress. Hope and her husband appearing on the stairs were dismissed hurriedly. Their presence would only complicate matters Matthew explained.

All that day and the following night Faith was in labour with the premature birth. Dr. Armstrong bustled in and out of the vicarage hourly, but Mercy never left her sister's side, whilst Alfred, helplessly impractical, offered earnest prayers, seldom rising from his knees.

Faith, a thin wraith, her face wet and grey with agony clung to Mercy when prolonged pains wracked her. She was, with each spasm, growing weaker and even her whispered words were painful.

"Look after Cissie and the baby for me, Mercy. I feel I am dying, promise me you will care for them."

"You are *not* going to die, dearest," Mercy cried fiercely, clutching the weak hands with her own firm brown ones. "Hang on to me; I shan't let you go. What would any of us do without you?"

A flicker of a smile crossed the wan face and the

doctor entering the room saw it.

"You can save her, my girl," he said to Mercy. "I am relying on your willpower if all else fails."

Another day dawned and when it seemed the tortured body could struggle no more, to the distraught watcher's relief a little boy was born to live but ten brief minutes.

Mercy's long unceasing vigil and stubborn refusal to accept defeat brought its reward. Alfred, his long face lined with misery, thanked God in His mercy for delivering his wife safely back into his keeping. He firmly believed it was his own devout prayers that saved her, but Dr. Armstrong, sharing a much needed drink with his old friend Matthew, assured him it was Mercy they had to thank for giving Faith the courage to survive.

Propped on her pillows, white and thin as a skeleton, the patient's first days of recovery were spent in inconsolable grief for her dead baby son. After that she accepted God's will, and listened gravely to Matthew's remarks. Dr. Armstrong predicted there would be no further children, and to wish for more would be wrong. Faith must now concentrate on regaining her health, for Alfred, Cissie and little Emily needed her. Her life had been blessedly saved and she must give thanks for that, for the anguish suffered by her husband, himself, and the rest of the family could never be endured again. She must be a dear good girl and recover quickly. When she was well enough it was his desire to send them all away to the sea for a beneficial holiday.

The house in Holly Walk seemed empty while Mercy was caring for the invalid and Matthew felt her absence keenly. The affection he had for Hope although still binding did not suffice. Without her husband, who had too soon gone, she was moody and irritable. He had sailed for Turkey during the dark days of Faith's crisis and Mercy regretted not saying goodbye to him.

The manuscript left behind Matthew found impressive. He spent many evenings in his library studying the closely written pages. It irked him that Mercy was absent at these times; there were many points he could have discussed with her and she would have appreciated so much the humour of the written word.

Hope was useless. He tried to interest her once or twice in the scripts, but she looked vague and bored although happy enough that her father was so enthusiastic about her husband's work.

The loss of his new born grandson was also a grief to Matthew and the doctor's ultimatum regarding further children for the young couple's sake caused him genuine sorrow. His own ambitions were thrust aside. With two other daughters now married a male heir for himself was still highly probable.

As the summer wore on disturbing news seeped into the town. War correspondents were bitterly blaming the Government for its apathy and attacking the ineffectual conduct and strategy of the War Office. It was not an infrequent sight now to see deep mourning in the streets, while a number of severely wounded men were being shipped back to England and the London hospitals.

How Charity was faring was a nagging worry to the family. Her letters had become more infrequent and rumours of frightful ills and pestilence were rife. Had the women succumbed to the misery of Scutari or had they been transferred into further depths of the Crimea, where a number of unpronounceable towns were said to be under siege?

Letters came from Miles, always short, sometimes written on crumpled filthy paper, quite often stained with what to Mercy's diligent eyes was blood. That the Hussars were faring badly seemed the accepted plight.

The one lucky enough to receive the most frequent and most rewarding letters was Hope. Her husband managed somehow to get news through regularly. She read snatches of interest out to them but frowned if he dwelt too long on unpleasant events.

Matthew was gratified to receive a letter from Paul himself containing information regarding an iron shortage on the battlefields, and warning Matthew to be cautious with his railroad stock. As a war correspondent he seemed more familiar with Army manoeuvres and positions than the troops themselves, and his news was disquieting. Their father revealed only the less frightening news to the girls and kept from them his own apprehension.

Although Faith was now beginning to put on

flesh, her dark shadowed eyes and white transparent skin needed the sun and fresh air to strengthen her for the winter. Matthew felt all the girls needed a change. Both Mercy and Hope, married yet without husbands, were leading cramped unnatural lives, so in August arrangements were made to transfer them all to Brighton.

Matthew drove them down himself. He had recently, having some substantial success with cotton shares, invested in a stately barouche and two chestnut mares. For comfort the new rubber tyres were a marked improvement and everyone felt the benefit of the smooth quieter ride.

The hotel was large and comfortably appointed on the sea front, with magnificent views of the sea. Matthew had no compunction at leaving the girls there, comfortably installed for a month.

How the little ones loved the sands. They were allowed to remove their tiny buttoned boots and white stockings and patter their feet in the gently lapping waves. They all sat on the shore, pretty light skirts spread about them like summer flowers, their parasols shading delicate skins from the sun's fiercest rays, though Mercy several times discarded hers to Faith's disapproval.

It was a time of transition, a time when each day floated dreamily by and only a distinct chill in the early twilight warned them summer was almost gone. Soon it would be time to return to Holly Walk. What would the winter bring? How long before the distant drums ceased? How long before Charity, Miles and the little known Paul, came home? With the pattern of each one's life changing their personal worlds would start anew.

The house had been depressingly silent for Matthew over the last few weeks and he looked forward with pleasure to the girls' return. The rustle of skirts, a tinkling music box, and faltering tunes on the piano had been sadly missed.

They arrived in a flurry of excitement, but in a few hours things were back to normal and it seemed they had never been gone.

Cheering news from Paul in December told them the war was speeding to its inevitable end, but although stimulating it brought none of their menfolk home for Christmas.

The manuscript left by Paul kept Matthew busily engaged in the long dark evenings and he took to reading passages to Hope and Mercy as they sat relaxing in the drawing-room after supper. Mercy delighted in probing into past history and puzzling a particular point out with her keen intellect, sharing her father's absorption. But to Hope's butterfly mind it was all a trifle tedious.

As the first daffodils appeared in spring, Mercy became aware more and more of Hope's restlessness. Several times she suggested outings together, fearful to what lengths boredom might drive her headstrong sister.

None of them knew that one July morning several months later a letter addressed to Matthew bearing a Portsmouth postmark would bring such stupendous events.

Neither girl noticed their father's reactions until a sharp exclamation alerted them and they saw dread in his face.

"What is it, Papa?" Mercy managed to falter.

Seeing their concern, he instantly put their minds at rest regarding their respective husbands. "Something concerning Charity has arisen in the most grievous manner," he told them. "I have an extraordinary letter from a person, posted in Portsmouth, which I shall read to you. It is dated earlier this month and commences in the oddest manner."

Matthew cleared his throat and Mercy guessed his agitation by the tremor in his voice.

"Dear Mr. Glover,
I am writing to tell you that your daughter Miss Charity Glover has arrived in Portsmouth today from the Crimea. I am sorry to tell you she is very bad, and not being able to look out for herself I have taken her over. She saw me through some bad times in Scutari and when other folk gave up she saved my life. I came across her again by accident a few weeks ago when we was being loaded into boats for England. She was in charge of another nurse, a Miss McCloud who died of typhoid on the boat. There was no one but me to look out for Miss Charity, so I took it on myself to see her safely home. Being injured myself I have finished my fighting days so I won't be going back to war. I was able to get her into hospital at Portsmouth but they can't keep her there, the beds is needed

for men wounded at Inkerman. I shall keep with her until you fetch her home, but she is very bad and you'd better be quick.
Yours truly
A. C. Wilkins. Sergeant."

They sat until the silence in the room became unbearable then both girls spoke at once, Hope through floods of tears, Mercy calm, but white-faced.

"Oh poor Charity...."

"Papa, how soon can we go?"

Matthew sat quietly brooding while after the outburst they waited silently for him to speak.

"I wonder if I should go alone."

"But you can't, Papa. She will need someone to attend to her and you cannot supervise everything and look after her as well. They will be far too short of nurses to allow one to travel with her. Please let me come," Mercy implored.

Matthew looked at Hope enquiringly.

"Come, my dear, dry your tears. Once she is home among us I am sure all will be well. If I take Mercy, I know I can rely on you to see a comfortable room and medical supplies are acquired for your sister. Contact Dr. Armstrong immediately and he will advise you."

Hope nodded. Matthew knew very well how the grim sights of an army hospital would be liable to send her into hysterics. That she could be trusted to organise things at this end he was confident, but he badly needed Mercy's strength to bolster his own jaded spirits. Recalling how gallantly she had rallied everyone during Faith's illness he believed she would act accordingly in this emergency.

He passed the letter over for them to see. It was ill-spelt and badly written, but the cry for help was sincere, and whoever the fellow was he evidently thought well enough of Charity to tend her until other help arrived.

Matthew ordered the barouche. It was wide enough to take Charity's little body across one seat padded with pillows and blankets. With medicines, brandy, eau-de-cologne—a feminine necessity Hope insisted on supplying from her own dressing-table—and a hamper of food, they were soon on their way. Archer was driving in case Mercy needed assistance with the patient on the return journey. But as they bowled along Matthew sat beside his servant, urging the mares to greater speed, a fearful growing anxiety eating into his heart.

They made good time to Winchester where a rest and change of horses was necessary. After a few short hours spent in a coaching house, refreshed by food and a brief sleep, their journey continued.

Darkening skies brought rain as they neared the coast. It had seemed to Mercy the longest day in the world. When the sea was sighted her head felt fit to burst with anxious anticipation and mingled joy at the thought of seeing her sister once again.

As they drew near the hospital the roads were

lined with vehicles and Archer had some difficulty in steering a clear path for the carriage. Gun carriages, army carts, haywains, farmers' wagons, were strewn in haphazard fashion. A few thin listless horses grazed nearby, but even as they advanced further carts laden with men drew up before them. Weary wounded men, with lifeless limbs, filthy bandages and rough hand-made crutches were assisted from the vehicles. Many were far beyond human help and now and again a gush of scarlet would spring unexpectedly from an unknown source. How many of the severely wounded survived the short distance from the docks to the hospital was a miracle.

To Mercy, the first sight of mangled bodies and gaping wounds made her heave. She turned away sharply and vomited into her handkerchief, thankful that Papa aloft could not see her and became fiercely determined to check her revulsion. What good would she be to Charity if the first sight of blood upset her?

The stench erupting from the carts was excruciating and Matthew, his face grim, climbed down to her side.

"You had better stay in the carriage I think. Archer is seeing to the mares. I will be back as soon as possible."

"No, Papa." She opened the door determinedly. "I am coming with you."

Hesitating, he looked at her set little chin and capitulated.

"Very well. If you insist."

They picked their way between lines of staggering soldiers, each supporting more badly wounded comrades, until they entered the hospital itself. Here the closely confined building made the smell unbearable and Mercy fought down her nausea with difficulty. Makeshift stretchers lay row upon row in the corridors whilst men lay pain-crazed, sweating, unwashed, waiting for the help which never seemed to come. Many were mercifully unconscious, thin blood-soaked rags barely covering their gaping wounds. Some called for water and looked beseechingly at Matthew and Mercy as they hurried by. Here and there a doctor, overworked, dazed with fatigue, toiled silently, and the swish of a skirt told a nurse was nigh. Mercy, eyes blinded with tears clung to her father's arm as they picked their way along, fearful of treading on the wounded, until they came to a ward filled with the wrecks of humanity where utter chaos reigned. Screams of pain rent the air, mingling with cries for release and the clink of medical instruments.

Matthew grimly held Mercy's arm in an agonising grip and managed by sheer force to stop a scurrying nurse. She carried a bowl half filled with blood and Mercy averted her eyes, afraid of the cowardly sickness again betraying her. Her father had to shout to make himself heard.

"I'm looking for Miss Glover. Miss Charity Glover."

The nurse shook her head and passed on as if in a trance. She must have been on duty for days thought Mercy, and was then suddenly aware of another voice shouting to her father.

"I am Wilkins, sir. I have been waiting for you. I'll take you to Miss Charity."

He was a little man; a livid scar slashed across his stubbled grimy face. His filthy beard and matted unkempt hair stank, while one sleeve swung loosely at his side. He said nothing more, but limping ahead took them swiftly through a side door and into a small hut. There were three cots side by side. Two bodies covered with grey army blankets lay on two of them but the third held a slight scarcely breathing bundle of fleshless bones.

The little man waved them quietly forward and they stood silent, looking down on the gentle, appealing, uncomplaining face of Charity.

SIXTEEN

Had it been possible for Matthew to hire one horse, let alone two, there was not a creature in the town free and capable of carrying the carriage back to Winchester. Apart from the tradesman's animals which understandingly they refused to part with, those not already acquired for the army were totally unfit to go between shafts.

There was no alternative but to wait for their weary horses to rest. Archer would take no responsibility for their condition if they ventured a step without at least six hours respite. As they were only hired animals their condition was far short of Matthew's thoroughbreds and he chafed at the delay in getting back to the coaching house when the reins of his own mares would once more be in his hands.

It was early dawn therefore when they set off after a few uncomfortable hours sleep snatched inside the barouche, far enough from the hospital for the heart-rending cries to escape their discerning ears.

Charity lay along one seat, padded by pillows, with warm blankets tucked around her. Mercy had brushed the tangled lice-infested hair away from her face and tied it up in a clean napkin. She was conscious and had acknowledged them immediately, giving a faint welcoming smile and promptly sighed herself into a deep sleep. Sergeant Wilkins was gratified.

"The first good sleep she's had for many a long day," he remarked brusquely.

Determined, in spite of his single arm on carrying her to the carriage, he tenderly laid her down, but she opened her eyes and murmured, "Thank you, Will. Don't go away."

He nodded a promise and dropped on the grass outside, not far from Archer, wrapped in a blanket and fitfully dozing.

Before leaving, Charity, refreshed from her sleep and a few sips of brandy Matthew insisted she take, startled them by requesting Sergeant Wilkins should accompany them back to the Midlands.

"I will explain later, Papa," she whispered. "But I cannot abandon him now. If it hadn't been for Will I would be dead, buried at the bottom of the sea."

Seeing her distress Matthew agreed, and the ragged lame veteran was hoisted onto the seat beside Archer, who, although as composed as ever, kept several inches between them and his nose towards the wind.

Mercy met her father's look over the recumbent

figure of the invalid. Both speculated on her survival of the journey and in their eyes was the unwilling truth. Charity was desperately ill. Her life hung on a feeble thread and only her extraordinary will power could pull her through.

Matthew could not erase from his mind the disgraceful conditions he had seen at Portsmouth. The atrocious way the troops were conveyed from ships to hospital disgusted him. He was determined to write a strong and vehement letter to *The Times*, which he did at a later date. The letter was given preference and printed in its entirety, scandalising many members of the Government but causing the War Office, unknown to him, to probe more closely into the welfare of their Army.

The fight for Charity's life was grim. She lay in her bed like a little wax doll, sleeping gently, her breathing scarcely audible. Sometimes a nervous rasping cough disturbed her, but more often she slept on hour after hour. Matthew, desperately afraid, suggested they bring a specialist from London. Dr. Armstrong, however, although perplexed, advised him to give her forty-eight hours. Worried himself about the persistent cough, he felt until she recovered from her collapse a complete examination of the patient was impossible. So little could be done. Once or twice she opened her eyes and sleepily looked into Mercy's anxious face. She was, in spite of her exhaustion, completely aware of her surroundings and her weak voice spoke softly.

"How wonderful it is to be home with you all. Is Will here? Make sure he is well cared for; I owe him so much."

Mercy assured her Sergeant Wilkins was in good hands. Archer had taken firm charge of him. Finding a spare room over the stables, he had supplied a truckle bed, blankets, clothing and other facilities for the war-torn soldier. Not before of course, having a word with the worthy doctor and obtaining from him a supply of evil smelling liquid to delouse the unhappy man. He was soaked in carbolic and heartily scrubbed by Simon and Archer under the garden pump until he emerged, his brown skin almost raw, but at least clean. A troublesome wound in his leg was treated and the stump of his arm inspected thoroughly for infection. A deep scarlet sabre slash across his face was more evident and frightening than ever, and everyone was amazed to find that, with the former mud in the thick hair removed, a thatch of snowy white appeared above his shrewd grey eyes.

Matthew for his own satisfaction naturally interrogated the man, learning his full name was Alexander Cromwell Wilkins, commonly known as Will. Other information he kept to himself, although a rising and falling of the voice suggested a Welsh lilt.

He had never married and previously been manservant to a succession of gentlemen. At the outbreak of war he had joined the Yeomanry in a burst of patriotic fervour. He had been engaged in fierce fighting at Balaclava and had become a medical orderly when too seriously wounded for further active service. By his organisation of the wounded at Scutari he had achieved the rank of sergeant and it was here he had come into contact with Charity, working with her and helping in the wards on many occasions. From Scutari he was sent to join a hospital ship and assist with the injured sailing for England. Here maimed and dying men, several of them suffering with typhoid—which later became rife on board—were attended by a few nurses of whom Charity was one. He, in spite of Matthew's probing, firmly belittled the part he had played in rescuing her, insisting anyone given the chance would have done likewise.

Matthew, impressed by the man's humility, instructed Archer to find him suitable work which least aggravated his infirmities. The maids were at first wary of him. But he, naturally a silent man, treated everyone in the kitchen courteously, never intruding unless invited, and gradually they came to accept him as one would a fierce looking but harmless dog.

Archer discovered at once how useful he was in the stables, how completely at home among the glossy high-spirited animals Matthew owned. He talked to them soothingly and with assurance, his voice far more tuned to the four-footed creatures than human beings.

In the subdued atmosphere inside the house a gradual change was taking place in Charity's condition. As the days went by she became more alert and was able to take refreshment and the nourishing broth Cook so gladly toiled to provide.

THE HOUSE IN HOLLY WALK

Her clothes had been burned in the garden incinerator and she was gently cleansed and perfumed to rid her nostrils of the stench Mercy felt sure would never leave her own. Hope had cut her hair to rid it of tangles and troublesome lice and as the dark little tufts stood out around the thin face she looked extraordinarily childlike.

Matthew was cross the first time he saw her.

"Did you have to do that?" he enquired angrily. "Her hair was so thick and beautiful."

"It was necessary Papa. Don't worry, it will soon grow again."

"Don't you think she looks better?" Mercy enquired.

They stood around her little white bed, those who loved her best. Matthew, Hope, Mercy and Faith, watching lovingly for any sign of improvement, anxiously awaiting the time when she would be able to sit by the open window and look onto the colourful garden.

When she was strong enough to be treated by a specialist from London, he was closeted for more than an hour in her room, and a private talk with her father followed. Afterwards Matthew raised no false hopes.

"She is very ill and both lungs are affected. She will have to be treated with the utmost care, kept well out of draughts, and the strictest medical attention must be observed."

"Couldn't she go abroad for a cure? People go to Switzerland for the treatment of consumption, don't they?"

"It is too late for that, travelling is out of the

question. Dr. May is astounded she survived the journey home."

"But surely she will be able to get up soon, now the warm days are here?"

"I sincerely hope so; it is up to us to spare no effort to get her well. This accursed war has much to answer for. Apart from taking our bravest men, it has taken the lives of our women too."

"She should never have gone," burst out Hope. "I can't understand why she wanted to go out to that disgusting place."

"The need was there. She *had* to go," Mercy answered soberly. "She believed the life God gave her was dedicated to that purpose, I think if she had a second chance she would do it again tomorrow."

They all, knowing the resolution of their sister, were inclined to agree. Mercy felt immensely depressed and went through the garden towards the river, thinking how pitiless life could be.

She was startled by a silent figure sitting on a grass verge in the silence of the noon sun. As he rose to his feet she saw it was Will, and his grey eyes sought her own as he spoke.

"Excuse me, Mrs. Finch. Will you please tell me what the doctor said about Miss Charity."

"It's not very good news I'm afraid, but we can only hope. Doctors can sometimes be wrong." She went on to give him the doctor's views.

A harsh note crept into his voice as he acknowledged her remarks and she had difficulty in hearing the muttered words. "If she dies there's nothing left for me."

"But she's not going to die, Will." She looked at the little man compassionately. "Dr. May says her lungs are affected and she has to be carefully nursed, but before the summer is over she will walk in her favourite place by the lily pond. If skill and prayer and her own will power can do it, it will be so."

His mouth creased up on the unscarred side, where no disfigurement prevented the tilt. It was the first time Mercy had seen him smile.

"You're a real lady, Mrs. Finch, just like Miss Charity." He paused. "Mrs. Cohen—" Something in her face prevented further speech, so he shrugged and said impulsively: "It does me 'eart good to know you're looking after 'er yourself."

As he turned away she noticed something partly concealed by the cap in his hand.

"What are you hiding there?" she asked.

He brought the object forward and she saw it was a knife, its ragged edge covered with rust.

"Why it looks like a kitchen knife."

"A butcher's knife more like. I found it buried in Minstrel's stable."

"Really?" She bent forward. It was stained and rough from disuse. "It's very like one Cook uses for cleaving the meat. I seem to remember she did replace one last summer."

"Last summer?" Will's eyes lifted swiftly then he looked down again at the weapon in his hand. "Ah well, things 'ave a habit of turning up in unexpected places. I were taking it to clean on the grinding stone."

"You do that. No doubt Cook will be glad to

have it back. Old tools are like old friends and cannot be replaced."

She watched his figure limp out of sight as Hope appeared at her side, frowning after him.

"What did *he* want? I don't like the way he hangs around the house and I can't understand Papa allowing him to stay."

"He works in the stables mostly and rarely comes near the house. But he is anxious about Charity naturally, everyone is."

Hope said nothing and together they walked slowly along.

"He is so ugly," Hope complained. "With that dreadful scar and horrible shuffling walk, he revolts me. But it isn't only that." She paused. "There is something about him I don't understand. I don't suppose you have noticed it, Mercy, but he stares at me in the oddest way."

"Oh rubbish, Hope! You think every man gives you flirtatious glances. You had better watch out when Paul comes back or else he'll be wild with jealousy."

"I don't mean that, stupid! He treats me to some very belligerent stares and his eyes flash alarmingly; sometimes I feel quite scared."

"Will's eyes flash? His are the mildest I have ever seen," Mercy laughed. She glanced at her sister thoughtfully. "I think you have been too long tied to the house and started imagining things. Why don't you ride over to Nancy's; the change will do you good. She must be hurt you have neglected her so long, and pregnancy isn't infectious you know. Besides you can tell her all about Charity's dramatic return. Don't worry about things here; Faith is coming in soon so we can manage beautifully."

Hope took her at her word and spent the afternoon with her friend. She was late returning, so late in fact that Mercy, to ease her father's mind, walked down to the gate in search of her.

As she looked out, half hidden by the laurels, she saw two figures silhouetted against the setting sun. One was Hope, walking the cob, bridle dangling in her hands; the other, short, thickset, awkward, could be no other than Will.

Astonished, Mercy stood, and their voices, although low, carried on the gentle breeze. It was impossible to hear their conversation, but sharp anger was in Will's voice, and Hope's rose furiously in that curiously shrill way it had when roused.

Mercy stood for a few moments, then returned to the house. The strange sight she had just seen puzzled her greatly. What had brought about a quarrel between those two? Why was Hope conversing with him at all when only a few hours earlier she had confessed her loathing for the man? Will, who was naturally reticent, would never have approached her unless there was some special reason behind it.

If only there wasn't this long impossible bridge between herself and Hope, a bridge that would never be crossed unless her sister admitted the truth, acknowledged her child and stopped the hysteria that arose every time the subject was mentioned. Nothing was left now between them; they were strangers, distant, polite, discussing domestic affairs attentively, but sharing only the unhappy problem of Charity. Everything else was void.

She still heard faithfully from Mrs. Boniface and all seemed well, but it was now six months since her honeymoon spent in London and it was too long to leave the child without more substantial contact.

SEVENTEEN

ON THE FIRST day Charity left her bed and was propped up in a chair by the window, bowls of late summer roses brought festivity to her room. The warm September air touched her cheeks, and Faith's children who had not been allowed in the sick room, stood beneath the window waving excitedly, while Gyp scampered around in bewildered confusion.

Beneath the huge chestnut tree a solid figure stood silently watching her white hands fluttering at the children. Seeing him, Charity's face broke into the old transfiguring smile and she spoke to Mercy at her side.

"I must speak to Will soon. Do you realise I have scarcely seen him since we returned? How long is it now?"

"Just over a month, but you needn't worry on his account. He asks after you every day and has made quite an impression on Archer who speaks highly of his work with the horses. He is devoted to them and Papa is very pleased."

"It is as I expected. I just cannot tell you what strength he had during that terrible journey back to England, no one could have consoled me more when Sister McCloud died."

Mercy was only half listening. She had noticed Hope crossing the grass suddenly stop at the sight of Will and return abruptly to the house. Without hesitation she encouraged her sister to talk.

"He seems reliable but is very reticent. What do you know of him apart from his war record?"

"Very little really. I do know he travelled extensively before enlisting, but he has never spoken of his private life. I do believe he is far more sensitive than people imagine and the monstrous sights he saw may have affected his nerves badly. No man escaping with his life after that violent disaster of the Light Brigade could remain unmoved however hard a veteran he may be, and Will is certainly not that."

"So you think there is another side of his nature we know nothing about?"

"Oh nothing to cause alarm, and nothing a spell of peace and quiet cannot cure. As soon as I am well enough to sit in the drawing-room I intend having a long talk with him. I see no reason why he shouldn't become a permanent part of the household, and I shall do everything to gain Papa's support."

It was only days after this that Charity, wax-like face tinged with a flush of expectation, made her first trip to the drawing-room. Mercy brought out for her debut the beautiful Indian shawl, and a tiny lace cap with fresh ribbons sitting atop the short wispy curls made her seem stylish indeed.

How happy everyone was. Even Cook climbed the stairs, no mean feat considering her painful bunions, but beaming with delight to see her young Miss so greatly improved, and the maids were allowed a peep. An aura of love and affection surrounded the smiling girl. The joy she felt inspired her to talk of her own recovery and how soon she would be returning to her work. Matthew hid the painful truth and remonstrated with her, explaining what strides must be made before even the lightest tasks could be undertaken. It was a strain for him seeing the hope in her eyes while visualising the future she planned.

That she found her slow progress irksome he accepted. What would she feel when she was forced to accept the inability to renew her former strenuous work? Frustration at her own weakness now often brought tears to her eyes.

"There is so much work to be done, Papa," she would tell him fretfully. "What time is wasted whilst I am lying here in comfort. Many hands are needed for nursing, when I think...."

"You all did your best. The little I saw of the nurses and their revolting tasks grieved me."

"But so few of us, Papa." She shook her head sadly. "So few."

Matthew with his perceptive mind saw a post-illness depression creeping over her and called a family consultation to seek some means of removing it. There was so little she could do physically and the long hours of immobility must be trying to one used to tripping about on tireless feet. Her hands although improving were often too weak to hold a pen so writing at length was an impossibility, and although the rough callouses were disappearing, needlework was as yet out of the question. They found whatever books would interest her and she would sit, her short-sighted eyes close to the page for hours. The despised little steel-rimmed spectacles had been lost long ago somewhere in the havoc of Scutari.

Mercy, remembering their former chat, suggested Will be brought up for a talk with her. Hope reacted violently.

"That fellow in the drawing-room. Certainly not. You cannot allow it Papa."

Astonished, Matthew raised his eyebrows.

"Why not? What possible objections could there be? I think it is a very good idea and am only surprised I failed to think of it myself." He paused, looking closely at Hope.

"Has the man been uncivil or disrespectful to you at all, or is there something in his conduct you have kept from me?"

Hope hesitated, then shook her head.

"Nothing. I just distrust him that's all. Oh, I wish Paul would come home."

"I am sure you wish that but you must not complain; you have been more than fortunate in receiving your share of correspondence, but Mercy has been waiting weeks for news of her husband. I must insist on you being a little more patient and considerate for others."

Hope said nothing but coloured and stabbed viciously at her needlework. Matthew was mystified by her behaviour, particularly over the last few days. She was short with everyone, and with a nervousness foreign to her nature seemed afraid of her own shadow. He realised at last there was a hard core in her, had unwillingly known it ever since the day she had run away with that Betteridge fellow. He had been deceiving himself into thinking the love and loyalty offered by the family would change her. Occasionally he wondered why she had married Paul Cohen. Was she genuinely fond of him, this man with the unusual qualities? It had surprised him that she, setting such store by personal appearance, should have accepted one with indifferent looks, unless, as he recently suspected, she had snatched at the first suitable man capable of impressing her family and friends.

However, his prime consideration now was Charity and he endorsed Mercy's plan regarding Wilkins.

"We will bring him up to the drawing-room tomorrow. I can arrange to be home about noon."

"I hope, Papa, you do not think it necessary for me to be present," Hope snapped.

"It is as you wish of course, but it would be churlish for us all to ignore the fellow. I am sure I can rely on you, Mercy."

As he left the room Mercy glanced at her sister and spoke quietly. "You seem extremely resentful of Will. I think we owe him a great service, most of all Charity's life."

"Well all right, but need we discuss it further. I

am heartily sick of Sergeant Wilkins, Papa, and—oh everything! If I see Dr. Armstrong's moon-whiskered face once more this week I think I shall explode. Nothing will be more welcome than bed just now, I feel so tired."

Biting back a swift retort Mercy noticed the weariness on her sister's face. There were deep lines on her brow and the blue eyes caught in the firelight held a glitter of something unknown. Could it be tears? She half rose from her seat.

"I do wish you'd tell me what's troubling you."

The other shrugged faintly and started to speak, her voice scarcely audible.

"I can't. Don't ever ask me. But, oh Mercy I'm afraid, so terribly afraid."

With a whisper of skirts the door closed behind her and Mercy knew the chance of ever hearing the truth had gone, perhaps for ever.

Wilkins diffidently entered the drawing-room the following afternoon his heavy boots sinking into the pastel carpet. Matthew approached him genially.

"Come in, Wilkins, you are very welcome. As you see my daughter is much improved and was eager to talk with you."

He handed the man a glass of port while Charity treated him to her grave smile.

Hope sat in the wide window seat fiddling with the tea cups and she glanced at the man distastefully before with murmured excuses she left the room. Will's eyes followed her sombrely and his stony silence troubled Mercy. There was something secretive between those two, something hostile and destructive. Perhaps she was the only person to sense it but whatever the cause an element of fear and enmity existed.

The voice of Charity had power to rouse the fellow however for he shook off his brooding reticence. The room soon echoed with animation and laughter as they recalled the many humorous episodes and ridiculous situations they had shared together. They spoke of harrowing moments more soberly, speaking of former comrades with regret. That this absurd crass little man could bring such life and vitality to the pointed little face before them gave the two watchers much satisfaction. It was a tonic the patient badly needed.

An accident to Gyp gave Mercy the opportunity of a long talk with Will. Her little dog had been hobbling about painfully for a couple of days and refused to let herself or anyone else investigate the cause. "Take him down to Will, Miss Mercy," Archer advised. "He just has a way with animals like no one else I know."

It was true. In no time at all, soothed by Will's voice and patted affectionally during the operation, a long ugly thorn was removed from the swollen paw, and healing liniment expertly applied.

"Let 'im rest a bit afore using his foot, Ma'am. Shall I carry 'im to the 'ouse for you?"

"No thank you, Will; he seems quite comfortable where he is at the moment."

Mercy looked at the dog stretched at ease on the straw-covered floor. She sat down on a wooden stool, for a fine drizzle was falling outside, warning them that the mists of November were near.

Will hovered uncertainly on the step, and she motioned him inside.

"There's something I want to ask you," she said.

"Yes, Mrs. Finch?"

The man walked over to a corner and began polishing a bridle. It was quiet except for the snorting of the mare at close quarters and the breathing of Gyp, now content.

In her straightforward way Mercy put her question bluntly.

"One evening I saw you talking with Mrs. Cohen. You both seemed angry. What was it about?"

There was no reply so she waited; it seemed one had to be patient with Will.

"Begging your pardon, Mrs. Finch, but I think it's none of your business."

She sighed. "Well *I* think it is because something else is worrying me. The other day when you were in the house the atmosphere until Mrs. Cohen left was quite absurd. Why was that?"

"I can't say, Ma'am, I didn't notice."

"Oh come, Will. You are not a fool; you know perfectly well what I mean. You must realise how puzzled I am."

He went on polishing steadily, but Mercy had seen the quick searching look he gave her.

"I don't think I could bear to sit here all day, but I intend to until you give me a satisfactory answer."

He dropped the polishing cloth and moved forward where the light from the door caught the raw scar giving his face a sinister look.

"I see you are a very stubborn young woman, and if you really want to know 'ow it is between your sister and me, I'll tell you. But you're not going to like what you 'ear."

"Let me be the judge of that. I may not be as brave and noble as Charity, but at least I am sensible enough to keep my own counsel and recognise the truth when I hear it."

Looking out, Will closed the stable door, leaving them scant visibility. He kept his voice low.

"If you 'eard us talking together you will realise it isn't the first time Mrs. Cohen and I 'ave met."

"Well, I was puzzled naturally, and although I didn't exactly hear your conversation I knew you were quarrelling. Where had you met before?"

"It isn't for me to question a young woman's morals, but two years ago one of my young gentlemen travelling abroad 'ad a companion."

Mercy gasped. "You mean Harry . . . Harry Betteridge?"

Will nodded. "I was his valet at Oxford and when 'e did the tour I went along with 'em. Mr. Betteridge said 'e couldn't do without me."

"I am sure he did. They would both be very fond of their own comforts."

"Yes, Ma'am. A kind and generous employer 'e was and a great favourite with the opposite sex. On this particular trip the lady 'e took were very pretty. You can guess 'ow shook up I was when I came 'ere to find she was Miss Charity's sister."

"It must have been a shock."

He nodded in the gloom. "I couldn't rightly believe it, but she wasn't one you would pass over. I knew from the start she was a lady though, not one of these flighty pieces a lot of the gentlemen picked up. Everyone noticed 'er looks and the stir she caused wherever she went until 'er condition became . . . er delicate."

Will coughed discreetly and Mercy breathed encouragingly, "I understand."

"The time came when she couldn't do much gallivanting about and I will say this for Mr. Betteridge 'e looked after 'er real well. 'E were dead set on 'er 'aving this baby, although begging your pardon, Ma'am, 'er being your sister and all, I couldn't say she were very 'appy about it 'erself. Well, nothing would stop it and 'ave it she did, in Switzerland. As soon as she were well enough to travel, which I was surprised to find was pretty soon, we came back to England. I saw them settled in London and then Mr. Betteridge with all 'is money gone and everything 'ad to part with me. I didn't want to leave him nor the baby, it was a right bonny little thing and Mr. Betteridge were that proud of it, but there was nothing we could do."

Mercy bent her head. The story, although already known, had again touched her deeply.

"And so . . . ?" she asked softly.

"Well, it were after that I joined the Army and got mixed up in this Crimea business. It wasn't until I brought Miss Charity 'ome that I set foot in England again. Then when I saw Mrs. Cohen—well Miss Charity's sister!"

"What did she tell you—about the baby I mean?"

"Well it was some days afore I 'ad a chance to catch 'er alone and, as I guessed, she never suspected who I was. Mr. Betteridge always called me Cromwell, that being my middle name. 'E said it were too noble a name to waste and somehow it stuck—'e liked his little joke did Mr. Betteridge. Folk began calling me Will again when I went to the war, and I weren't a bad looking chap afore a sabre cut my face in 'alf and my arm were blown off. It's little wonder the lady didn't recognise me and when I did make myself known she nearly fainted with fright. I meant her no 'arm, I was just enquiring about Mr. Betteridge and the baby."

"Oh God. Harry! . . . You didn't know about that?"

"No, Ma'am, I didn't, and Mrs. Cohen didn't tell me neither. She simply told me she 'ad left Mr. Betteridge and come home; she said the baby was being taken care of. I thought it funny it weren't 'ere with 'er and the family but she said it was in London with its father. She said Mr. Betteridge loved the little chap so much he couldn't bear to part with 'im, so she had given him up. Very sorrowful she was."

The tears were now glistening in Mercy's eyes. Hope, a deceiver still, even now lying for her own ends. She felt a bitter sadness that her sister could sink so low, but at least the baby's identity was now established.

"Was that the evening I saw you on the hill?" she asked.

"No, that was a few days later after I'd settled in as the new stable 'and. I'd been down to the town for a drink and it were there I'd got chatting to a local chap and 'e tells me about the murder. I couldn't credit it were my young gentleman, Mrs. Finch. 'E 'ad always been so flash and happy, loving life so much."

"I know what you mean. Poor Harry, it was a dreadful affair. They never found the murderer you know."

"So I believe. Well, anyway it were that night Mrs. Cohen passed me on her mare going 'ome and I called her to stop. That was the time you saw us, Ma'am, and I was railing 'er about keeping the murder a secret. She made excuses, said she thought it would upset me. You know your sister, Mrs. Finch; you know 'ow she can twist anything to make 'er own side right and all the world wrong. Anyway she told me to mind my own business, to keep out of 'er affairs and if I interfered she would see I got dismissal from my job."

"Oh, Will. What can I say?"

"What is there to say, Ma'am? I couldn't bear to leave 'ere just yet. I know Miss Charity's days are numbered, but while she's still alive I want to stay near so I've kept everything to myself. It surprised me that I never once 'eard Mrs. Cohen's baby mentioned in the kitchen. I was a bit worried at first until it dawned on me 'is birth must 'ave been kept from everybody. If you 'adn't been so insistent I wouldn't 'ave told you, but I can tell by your face it were no surprise to you."

"I have known about the baby for some time. He is a dear little fellow and well cared for in London. My husband and I saw him earlier in the year so don't fret on his account. When this wretched war is over and Miles returns home we intend making other arrangements."

She stood up and straightened her shoulders.

"You know, Will, I feel for the first time since my husband left I have a friend in this troublesome business. Thank you for being so open and frank with me."

"Well, I must tell you, Ma'am, that next to Miss Charity you are the greatest lady I ever met. One evening when I went to seek out Mr. Betteridge's grave I saw you putting flowers there. 'E deserved some flowers did my young gentleman; 'e loved colour and laughter and all that was bright."

Mercy sighed. "It seems so long since it happened, and yet only just over a year."

"Not too long for the murderer yet to be found and I intend to try. If the constable 'asn't got time to dig into what's past, I 'ave. My work keeps me busy all day, but I 'ave the nights, and the nights is long and lonely, Ma'am. One day I shall find whoever did that terrible thing. I shall never give up till it's done."

Mercy left the stable. She felt tired, but her heart was lighter. Under the confusion of her thoughts was the firm conviction that Will, with the dogged determination of a battle-scarred little bulldog, would worry and probe into the facts of Harry's death until there was nothing left but the truth.

EIGHTEEN

WITH THE WAR still dragging on Christmas of 1855 drew near, and expectations of a reunion with their husbands seemed to the girls remote.

Hope's letters from Paul were enlightening. She was slightly aggrieved at Matthew's eagerness to learn their contents. Secretly she did think Paul harped a bit on the war, and would have preferred more intimacy with a little sentimental poetry for herself alone. However he was extremely optimistic and the satanic news that a year ago appeared so depressingly in *The Times* was gone. Now one could, she felt, look forward to something more lively in the not too distant future.

Miles also managed to write, but less frequently. Mercy, more patient than her sister, read his letters over and over, keeping to herself the comforting warmth of his love, thrusting depression aside, supremely confident in the knowledge that her husband would one day without warning come through the door as explosive and radiant as before.

THE HOUSE IN HOLLY WALK

December fourteenth was Charity's birthday so Christmas plans were abandoned and a celebration party arranged. Matthew wished it to be strictly a family affair with no over excitement to harm the invalid.

A special tea was prepared in the drawing-room and Charity quietly content sat with those who loved her. She opened her gifts and was as delighted with the homemade posies thrust into her lap by her two small nieces as with the expensive French fan from Matthew.

She lay back in her chair in the quiet of the evening and spoke to her father wistfully.

"Oh Papa, I do so want to get well." She showed him a letter received with her birthday congratulations that morning. "Look, they are keeping a place for me with Miss Stanley's party. There will be fifty women sailing for the Dardenelles soon after Christmas. I understand that things are changing rapidly out there, and the medical authorities are actually welcoming women nurses now." She paused and murmured half to herself. "So Miss Nightingale's fight in spite of everything has not been in vain. I must get well. I *must*."

Matthew knew letters coming frequently from old colleagues and associates kept the girl's unquenchable spirit alive, and tonight he blamed the unoffending one for the high colour in his daughter's cheeks. It might of course be the bright fire, for the room appeared unbearably hot, but obeying doctor's instructions an even temperature was observed, and the unusually mild and deceptive weather could play strange tricks on the unwary. It was with a troubled mind however he gave her an encouraging smile, and firmly bringing the party to a close, saw her settled again in her quiet room.

When the house was still, he sat in his library pondering over life's little ironies and an unreasonable melancholy depressed him. He who cared not a jot for premonitions was aware of an unknown fear moaning like a wind through the house. It was fortunate that he had business in London pending, and when he returned in a few days time he trusted the unwelcome ghosts would be gone.

It was evident to Mercy soon after her father's departure however that Charity was far from well. She slept until noon and then awoke in a bath of perspiration, complaining apologetically of a sore throat. The colour had left her face, and she, who only yesterday had seemed so vivacious, lay waxen and still, her regular cough harsh and dry. After a hurried consultation the sisters wasted no time in sending for Dr. Armstrong. He was located at the vicarage where Faith had called him to Emily who had been fretful and tiresome at the party. The child was covered with a rash and feverish, so Faith could not leave her, but promised to come over as soon as possible.

Mercy and Hope faced a grave doctor alone.

"Your sister is suffering from a severe chill," he informed them. "She must have attention at all times. Keep a good fire burning in her room and windows and doors tightly shut. I have prepared a soothing draught for her, but try to get her to take a little light food. How long will your father be away?"

They told him and he frowned worriedly.

"But surely there is no need for alarm," Hope cried anxiously. "She seemed perfectly well yesterday at her party."

He nodded. "Yes. Well, perhaps a little over-excitement may have brought the rise in temperature; however you must not forget the slightest indisposition to a person in your sister's state can very quickly give concern. At the moment there is little to worry about, just do as I say. I have a few calls to make, but will be back to see her again shortly."

The temperature did not subside and soon the whole house was aware of acute anxiety. Faith's visit coincided with the doctor's and he immediately ordered her away.

"You shouldn't be here now," he barked sharply. "Get back to your child." His voice softened as he saw her distressed look and he patted her arm. "I am sorry, Faith, but we cannot risk any infection reaching the sickroom here. What ails little Emily is probably only a childish complaint; I shall know later, but go away now."

With tear-filled eyes Faith left and he called the other two girls together.

"I don't wish to alarm you unduly, but I am perplexed at your sister's condition. If by morning it worsens I shall have to send to London for further advice, but let us hope that will not be necessary. I shall require someone to sit with her indefinitely. You should be able to arrange that between you, and your parlour maid—what's her name—Amy?—seems a sensible wench, get her to assist. If you need me at any time during the night, send without hesitation. Her fever may fluctuate, but the room must be kept at an even temperature and whichever of you does the night duty, keep alert. Understand?"

Stunned, the girls assented. Hope's eyes were wide with fright as they watched him leave. "Shouldn't we get in touch with Papa?"

Thrusting down a rising panic, Mercy answered: "Not yet. We must wait until tomorrow morning. I doubt if he has reached his hotel yet. Dr. Armstrong will tell us if it is necessary. I shall sit up myself tonight."

Between them they arranged a schedule and Mercy went below stairs to face a battery of frightened questions and tears from the staff. All volunteered help and she recruited Amy for the following day. Archer informed her the gig was ready for instant use should the need arise.

"We must hope it won't come to that," Mercy told him soberly and, sighting Will outside the kitchen door, called to him. He looked at her dumbly, his eyes distraught. "Let me do something please, Mrs. Finch. I don't care what I do as long as I can help."

"There is nothing at all at the moment, Will."

She looked compassionately at the bowed shoulders and beckoned him into the yard. "Moping won't help either. You know better than any of us what she has previously been through and there must have been worse moments than these. You know her courage never failed and I am sure it won't now. You've got to pray, Will. If she realises how urgently we are all praying for her she'll never dare give up."

The long night passed and Charity slept fitfully. By morning the fever was less apparent and although her forehead still glistened ominously, her breathing seemed easier and her cough less distressing. She apologised for causing them all such concern and despite difficulty in swallowing, took some broth and lay quietly inert, her white face composed, the froth of little dark curls surrounding her head like a halo.

When the doctor called in the early morning he was obviously relieved at her improvement. He assured the girls that although Charity was still gravely ill, her condition was less serious. She was not of course to be left and his frequent calls during the day told them the crisis was not yet over. He felt that Matthew's presence was not now necessary and they could relax, without becoming too complacent.

Mercy slept during the morning and awoke to find Will wandering under her window. She gave him a reassuring wave and watched him hobble away with a lighter step.

It was diagnosed that Faith's youngest child had

measles, and Cissie too had become infected. Neither parent could visit Holly Walk for fear of contaminating the patient, but news of Charity's progress was sent to the vicarage daily.

Acting as temporary nurses the girls worked diligently and by the third day considered the crisis was over. Although the dispirited feeling had vanished it would be some days before the normal bustle of the house was restored. Just as things seemed easier Amy had the misfortune to fall downstairs while carrying hot soup, and suffered a badly scalded leg. This meant more worry for the girls for although Polly did her share of daytime nursing neither of them felt she was capable of handling the vulnerable night hours. She had an irresistible tendency to doze off at any time and this unreliable habit could not be ignored.

Dr. Armstrong informed them that things were progressing so favourably they could relax their rigid routine, and after one more night this duty could cease. It was Hope's turn but Mercy, seeing her weariness, offered to do the duty instead, only to receive a defiant snap.

"No, I shall do it. I don't want it said I've failed in my share of responsibility."

"I didn't mean it that way," Mercy protested, "but you look so overwrought . . . ."

"Well, thank you! I know I must look a hag without you reminding me. You don't look so good yourself in spite of being three years younger."

Seeing the other's hurt face her voice softened, but she turned away irritably.

"Oh fiddlesticks, Mercy, I am quite capable of managing one more night. Thank goodness this will be the last; the thought of Papa returning tomorrow is like a tonic." She paused. "There is one thing you can do for me though. Keep that persistent horrible little stable hand away from the garden. Whenever I look out he is gazing up at the window. He's beginning to get on my nerves."

The night came on, long and black and still, but as Mercy went to her room she saw a bright new moon. It was she felt, an omen of hope and expectation, as fresh and sparkling as the frost it brought to settle softly on the skeleton trees.

She awoke to a crescendo of noise. She had been dreaming of Miles, a terrifying dream, where he had drifted further and further away from her on a red sea, a red disturbing unknown sea. Her face was cold when she opened her eyes and she thought the screams were her own. But they went on and on and suddenly she knew with sickening shock it was Hope. Instantly she was out of bed dragging her wrapper with her as she raced along the corridor to Charity's room.

Hope was swaying in the doorway, her mouth open to shriek again. Swiftly Mercy slapped her hard across the face and pushed past her into the room. As she gazed at the ashen face on the pillow, she knew.

Hope choked and gasped incoherently. "I must have dozed, I don't know—I woke up and she was coughing. I went to get water and suddenly—oh God!" She clapped her hand over her mouth muttering. "She started to cough—she must have been coughing—I don't know—I was asleep. And then there was this rush—this blood." She retched suddenly and her eyes dilated and Mercy felt herself beginning to shake, with her trembling legs giving way.

Hope was still gibbering. "She's dead isn't she? She died when she was coughing."

"Oh hush," snapped Mercy fiercely, clutching the bedpost for support. "We must send Archer for Dr. Armstrong. Where *is* Archer? Surely he must have heard . . ."

She turned as a figure appeared in the doorway and cried with relief.

"Oh, Will, thank God. Find help at once, will you?"

With menace the squat little figure advanced into the room closing the door behind him.

"It's no use; Archer's gone to meet the master's train."

For the first time Mercy looked at the man's face; his breath was coming thick and fast and the scar stood angrily clear. There was a fanatical gleam in his eyes. Falteringly she questioned him, terribly afraid.

"What are you doing? Will, Will . . . ?"

He ignored her and walking to the bed like a sleepwalker looked down at Charity. The sudden silence was far worse than the previous hysterical screaming. Turning from the bed with his curious shuffling gait he approached the now sobbing Hope. When he spoke his voice was painfully clear.

THE HOUSE IN HOLLY WALK

"You let 'er die. You killed 'er as surely as if your own hands had choked 'er."

Hope shrank away from the glowering figure bending over her.

"No, no, I couldn't help . . . ."

"You killed 'er," Will's voice lashed out with hatred. "I 'eard what you said: you were asleep when she died. You were supposed to be watching 'er and you let 'er die. But this is your second murder, my fine lady, it's nothing new to you is it . . . *is it?*"

Mercy rushed across to her terrified sister.

"Stop it. Stop it, Will, what are you saying? Go and get help immediately."

"This is the first time I 'ave disobeyed your orders, Mrs. Finch, and you don't need me to tell you it's too late for 'elping Miss Charity. Someone will come soon I daresay, but not afore I've done the job I came to do. I've got to avenge her death and that of my young gentleman. You may as well know that *she* killed 'im as well." He pointed at Hope. "Oh yes, your dear pretty sister has other blood besides this on her 'ands. She killed Mr. Betteridge without a doubt, after she ruined 'is life."

He gave a short sharp laugh. He's insane, thought Mercy; the shock has turned his brain. Oh God, besides the horror of Charity's death she had a madman to deal with too.

She edged towards the door, but his bulk barred her way. His laugh had died but the even tenor of his voice did not falter.

"I've no wish to 'urt you, Ma'am, but I shall not 'esitate if I 'ave to. Your sister must pay for the evil she's done, the two lives she's taken. Miss Charity could 'ave been saved if she'd done 'er duty."

He held her elbow in the steely grasp of his one arm and she was firmly propelled towards the bed. In that instant she saw for the first time, the knife. It was the old kitchen knife he had unearthed from Minstrel's stable. Its now polished steel gleamed wickedly in the flickering candlelight and she struggled furiously only to find his grip relentless and the knife against her throat.

She found her voice and it was dry with urgency.

"Listen to me. Please, please listen. What would Charity think if she knew how you are behaving? She had confidence in you, she cared about you, Will, about the hardships you've endured. She was so anxious you should have a better life."

Frantically she sought for words to reach him. "It can't really be you, planning to take away a life. . . ."

"I 'ave taken many a good life in battle, men whose lives were worth more than that of your sister, I'll swear."

Seeing out of the corner of her eye that Hope had mercifully fainted, Mercy stood her ground, playing for time. Why hadn't the servants heard their screams? Although Amy and Cook were incapable of climbing the stairs, one of the others must surely have heard. Her only hope was Papa. How long before he and Archer arrived home?

She continued talking. "But the only wrong Hope did was to fall asleep. And as for killing

Harry, you are terribly wrong. Even had such a thing been physically possible, she would faint at the first sight of blood."

"There's a side to that young woman you've never even seen, Ma'am, and don't forget that Mr. Betteridge never stopped caring for 'er. An hour or so's loving on the river bank would drain the very 'eart out of 'im. A thing like this," he waved the knife under her eyes savagely, "could be 'id in her petticoats easy, and afore 'e was aware it were done. She deserves to die by the weapon she used 'erself, I'm only sorry she ain't conscious to know the revenge I'm taking."

His wary eyes never left her face.

"Now, Mrs. Finch, I don't wish you to witness the murder of your sister so if you will lie down by Miss Charity, 'er quiet little body won't hurt you. Somehow I think she'd take it kindly like, knowing you were there beside 'er. It's no good crying out; I took the liberty of locking up the kitchen quarters so no one can 'elp you now."

"No, no..." Mercy's voice rose to a desperate shriek and he hit her then. It was a sharp stunning blow that sent her reeling into oblivion. She never knew how gently and with what sorrow he carried her to the bed where he covered her completely with the pink satin quilt.

When she recovered she found herself lying beside Charity, ashen and cold. She fought the rushing in her ears as memory came flooding back and struggling to rise was numb with disbelief. It was still with the still finality of death, and Will stood motionless against the facing wall.

"It's over," he said quietly.

She forced herself to look at Hope lying across the couch, her face chalk-white, hair spread like a gold crest. There was surprisingly little blood, just a neat small wound in her chest.

"She's dead," whispered Mercy hollowly.

"I 'ope so. You can call the others now."

He sat down woodenly on one of the little gilt chairs, head bent forward hopelessly, the knife still in his hand.

So Matthew and Archer in the pale light of dawn came upon this macabre sight. Charity and Hope dead, and Mercy in a state of stupefied shock.

Like a stone, Sergeant Wilkins sat, waiting with dumb patience for the constable to take him away.

With quiet efficiency Faith dispatched Polly to the vicarage and came to Holly Walk. She and Alfred between them brought some semblance of order to that distraught house.

Three years as a vicar's wife had taught Faith many things, not the least to keep a cool head in emergency and face adversity unflinchingly. She had met death in many forms, the vicar's lot being to succour his flock in all circumstances, and had, in her official capacity performed many deeds, even laying out dead bodies, an office of which Matthew, had he known, would have sternly disapproved. Although still gentle and easily moved, a resolute strength was developing her character. She earnestly and sensibly believed that the dead were peacefully resting in Heaven, but the sorrowing ones on earth were those in need of consolation.

She concentrated fully on Mercy believing, perhaps mistakenly, that Alfred could cherish her father. She kept the dazed girl in bed strictly sedated until the distressing funerals were over and the shocked horrified town had ceased to pry, however sympathetically, into their affairs.

The first snowdrops and aconites were peeping through the winter soil before Mercy recovered from her traumatic experience, and a tremor shook her regained control one day as Faith handed over a letter.

"I have kept it until I felt you were in a fit state to receive it," she said quietly.

Half fearfully Mercy looked at the envelope instantly thinking of Miles, but seeing it was Hope's handwriting she looked up enquiringly.

"She left it with me some months ago," Faith explained, "insisting carelessly, in her usual flippant way, that should anything unforeseen happen to her, it was for you alone. I think you are well enough now to accept it, but promise me whatever it contains you will treat it calmly. Remember nothing can hurt her now."

After she had gone Mercy sat with the letter unopened in her hands, a strange unwillingness to learn its contents swept over her, but it was not for her to disregard her duty.

"Dearest Mercy," it read, "I have no doubt the day will come when this letter will be placed in your hands, and the premonition I feel will not be unfounded. It may never be necessary for you to see it, if as I hope, Paul returns safely from the war and we can leave this place to continue our lives without the fear of past misconduct spoiling it. However since a man who was once Harry's valet and knows all my secrets came into our home, you will understand the dread that has caused me to write this confession. I mean of course Sergeant Wilkins and much as it will surprise you this statement is perfectly true.

I shall start by telling you the story you have so persistently believed about me bearing a child is true. I *did* have a son by Harry and he is, I understand, lodged in London. You probably know more about this arrangement than I do myself as I never had the slightest interest in him. He is solely and completely Harry's child and has no place whatever in my affections.

The other confession I have to make is far more serious and will I know shock you considerably, but it is a confession I must, if I am to have any hope of Heaven, disclose. It was I who killed Harry, I alone did that dreadful deed the police have been so long investigating.

He came to the house while you and Papa were in London, and caught me in the garden. No one else had the slightest suspicion but he insisted we talk together and to satisfy him I arranged a meeting the same evening by the river. I was determined he should not reenter my life and again spoil whatever chances I might have of finding happiness. How could I ever hope to marry and have a home of my own if he continued to appear every now and then to destroy it all?

We met and he tried to persuade me to return to him but I knew I could never do that. He did not threaten me, in fact I was astonished to learn he still loved me, at least he *said* he did and I suppose it is possible. I am inclined to believe however he just wanted a mother for the child and this I would not consider; I was afraid he would bring the boy to the house and Papa would disown me again. I killed him with the kitchen knife by sudden attack as he lay dozing in the grass. There was no struggle as I struck violently and in exactly the right spot. I felt no regret at the time for the shocking thing I had done, and even had another been arrested I doubt if I ever would have confessed.

Dear Mercy, you have always been my friend as well as my sister and the hurt I have felt over the present friction between us has wounded me deeply. I have thought so often lately of the secrets we shared when we were innocent and young. You were closer to me than either of the others and although Charity is an angel from Heaven, you I feel, are human enough to forgive and perhaps shed a few tears for all that has gone.

I would like Papa to know about the child. It may compensate in some way for losing me so shamefully, as undoubtedly I shall be lost if this letter is ever opened.

Whether you tell him I am a murderess, I leave to your discretion.

Try to think of me kindly sometimes.

    Ever your loving sister
     Hope."

NINETEEN

HE SAT ON top of the stile, a solitary pensive figure —greatly changed during the last eighteen months.

Outwardly there was little to see. Added grey in his rich brown hair and a wariness in the shadowed eyes might strike a keen observer, but inwardly he was scarred. Scarred for ever by the burden of memory. Haunted by that unspeakable night when he returned home to a holocaust of horror. For months afterwards he experienced no peace and spent sleepless nights cursing the day his open door had received a madman.

Admittedly justice had been done: Wilkins was arrested, tried, and eventually hanged for the murder of his daughter. Matthew, in spite of the hatred in his heart, had marvelled at the fellow's behaviour in the dock. Silently he stood erect, offering no defence, waiting expectantly for his sentence. When being led away, he lifted his head and looked Matthew straight in the eyes. Confounded he saw the pity there was for himself, Matthew the tormented, but he bowed his head and cursed the villain's soul to Hell.

Bitterly he reproached himself for putting his business affairs before the family and being absent during those disastrous days. Although the tragedy of Hope's murder could not have been anticipated, Charity's precarious health should have been warning enough and never could his own neglect be forgiven. Almost deranged, he had shut himself away, refusing in his misery access to anyone but Archer.

The arrival of Lydia from India in January had been his salvation. Horrified and deeply sympathetic his sister had nevertheless angrily remonstrated with him for his neglect of his youngest daughter. She, who after the first few weeks of depression, had taken control of the silent house.

Soon, Lydia had whisked them both away to Richmond for an indefinite stay. There in the sanctuary of his sister's peaceful home, Matthew came to terms with himself, and resignedly settled down to life and its extremities.

When they returned at last to Holly Walk, he realised his increasing dependence on Mercy. In comparison with the others, prim Faith, angelic Charity, and gay flirtatious Hope, he had accepted her as guileless, simple, free as the air. But it had taken Lydia to point out her stauncher qualities, to reveal to him the joy of Mercy, amiable, unchanging, too fond of animals, not particularly clever— Mercy, the ordinary one. Lydia saw to it that Matthew appreciated her. Her sharp tongue accused him of self pity and forced him to acknowledge the one who silently grieving, with the added anxiety of a husband still at war, had shouldered the burden that should have been his.

The plain speaking of his sister had jolted Matthew from his apathy and, despising his own former weakness, he tenderly fostered the girl until she shed the tightness of her reserve, and to his pleasure began to confide in him in the old familiar way. Within a few days she revealed the whole story of Hope's abandoned child. Astounded as he was, a nervous eagerness engulfed Matthew as together they boarded an early London train.

Only the presence of Mrs. Boniface kept his emotions under control as he gazed for the first time on his dead daughter's son. Those eyes, blue and innocent as Hope's had once been, captured his heart and without hesitation he elatedly brought the boy home. Home, to Holly Walk where the child's laughter would bring new life to a house in danger of becoming a tomb.

Now he climbed from the stile, leaving the churchyard and a daily visit to his daughters' graves. Together they lay in the shadow of All Souls, where a simple headstone gleamed in the sun and the grassy mound was invariably ablaze with flowers.

The Treaty of Paris thankfully signed in March of this year had brought the Crimean war to a close. Miles had returned, sound of limb but thinner, the young boyish look gone. In its place was the face of a man, composed, with watchful eyes, ready to forget the past futile years, content to settle down happily with his much loved wife. Mercy, now beautiful in a new maturity, was looking forward to the birth of their first child. Only too soon they would be sailing for India where Miles was to rejoin his regiment, and the irreplaceable presence of Mercy gone.

Paul Cohen had never returned. With several of his colleagues he was drowned in the Bosporus when their boat was struck by an enemy shell. Matthew still had his manuscript and although it was unfinished, intended publishing it, hoping to bring posthumous acclaim for the brilliant young writer.

Of Charity there was nothing but the undying memory of selfless devotion to a cause. Only a letter of consolation received after her death from Miss Nightingale was revered and proudly displayed. Matthew felt her true memorial was a compulsive tenderness bequeathed to the family she loved.

Approaching the gate of his home he paused at the picture before him. A quick businesslike figure appeared from the house bearing with ease a laden tea tray. With his family gone a housekeeper was now a necessity and this brisk, bird-like little woman with an extraordinary accent Lydia had found in London.

Faith was supervising tea under the elm. Both she and Mercy had discarded the gloomy black of mourning, and although avoiding bright dresses, they wore the delicate colours that suited the summer day.

As he crossed the grass, Jonathan flashed into view hanging on to Gyp's tail, while Cissie and Emily giggled delightedly. When the child saw his grandfather he raced forward and Matthew lifted him high with joy. Poor foolish Hope, how could she have doubted his love for her son? Although her life had been so tragically wrecked by the boy's father she had left behind this priceless legacy. It mattered not that his name had once been obscure; from the day the child entered Matthew's life he was known as Jonathan Glover.

Surprisingly Betteridge's murderer had never been caught. The case no longer caused speculation and was presumably closed. Any connection that Harry had once formed with his own family was now severed and the child was completely his —his to plan for and for him he would prepare a future as bright as the colour in the boy's cheeks.

Life still had much to offer. With the children clambering around him, Matthew knew that his house would again respond to youth's vitality as light running steps echoed up and down the stairs, and laughter would return once more to the house in Holly Walk.

There are a lot more where this one came from!

ORDER your FREE catalog of ACE paperbacks here. We have hundreds of inexpensive books where this one came from priced from 75¢ to $2.50. Now you can read all the books you have always wanted to at tremendous savings. Order your *free* catalog of ACE paperbacks now.

ACE BOOKS • P.O. Box 690, Rockville Centre, N.Y. 11571

Don't Miss these Ace Romance Bestsellers!

———— #75157 **SAVAGE SURRENDER** $1.95
The million-copy bestseller by Natasha Peters, author of Dangerous Obsession.

———— #29802 **GOLD MOUNTAIN** $1.95

———— #88965 **WILD VALLEY** $1.95
Two vivid and exciting novels by Phoenix Island author, Charlotte Paul.

———— #80040 **TENDER TORMENT** $1.95
A sweeping romantic saga in the Dangerous Obsession tradition.

Available wherever paperbacks are sold or use this coupon.

 ace books,
Book Mailing Service, P.O. Box 690, Rockville Centre, N.Y. 11571

Please send me titles checked above.

I enclose $.............. Add 50¢ handling fee per copy.

Name ....

Address ....

City.................... State............. Zip........

74B